NOW

THEN

AND

IN BETWEEN

Ashiq Sulfikar

FanatiXx Publication

Ashiq Sulfikar

FanatiXx® Publication

AM/56, Basanti Colony, Rourkela 769012, Odisha

ISO 9001:2015 Certified

By: Ashiq Sulfikar

ISBN: 978-93-5605-241-3
Book: Now then and in between
Price: INR 199/-
Cover By: Noorleen Kaur Bhatia
Printing By: BooksClub.in

DISCLAIMER

Ashiq Sulfikar

ACKNOWLEDGEMENT

When it comes to family, gratitude is a delicate feeling. My current viewpoint is founded on my family. Taking this chance, I'd like to thank my parents, Sulfikar K.C. and Bushra Sulfikar, and pay tribute to my beloved late brother, Chiku Sulfikar.

Without my friend Jyothilekshmi, this book wouldn't shine as brightly. Her unfailing support lighted my path like a beautiful chandelier throughout my writing trip.

I am grateful to Balkees Hameed for teaching me to the complexities and bright shades of screenplay writing while I was imprisoned by the darkness of unfamiliar words.

My sincere appreciation goes out to Purva Puri and Khushali Gadhi for providing outstanding editing support. They lit up this book with a rainbow of vivid phrases, like glistening stars.

Alfiya Sulaiman, Akshat Lakhe, and Noorleen made the cover design and final touches in the same way that a scent drifts through night blossoms.

I express gratitude to the supreme scriptwriter, Almighty God, for His unending stream of blessings, enriching my life's journey.

About the Author

Ashiq Sulfikar is an Indian author who opted for a hiatus from his career to pursue his passion for writing. Drawing from life experiences, he has developed a profound understanding of the emotions and needs of others, shaping his distinctive writing style. His literary focus revolves around themes of happiness, romance, and mystery, brought to life through engaging characters and compelling stories. Ashiq's writing possesses a unique charm that captivates readers, leaving a lasting impression. He believes in the power of perseverance, encouraging readers to maintain faith in their dreams, as success will inevitably come with patience and hard work. His works are infused with life, capturing elements from personal encounters while traveling and the people he has met. These nuances are woven throughout his writing, creating a rich tapestry of storytelling.

Contents

vi

PROLOGUE 3

PART 1 11

PART 2 27

PART 3 42

PART 4 77

PART 5 94

PART 6 144

Let's ponder over a thought tonight, not of love but of God – of why he makes children starve.

| PROLOGUE

The sun's rays filtered through the clouds. Making way for a new day, marking new beginnings, and promising more adventures. I opened my eyes to the beautiful morning sun, shining high and bright in the sky. Streaks of golden rays spanned the blue sky as another beautiful day unfolded before me. A warm breeze flew by, carrying the happy chirps of birds along. Morning rays poured into my bedroom through the window as I squinted my eyes at its light. A small fly was buzzing up and down by the glass that lined the window, trying to get out. It felt so refreshing and homey to wake up to the caress of sun rays rather than the unceasing screech of an alarm clock. My body squealed with unexplainable joy at the warmth, making it almost impossible to leave the bed. I rubbed my eyes, stretched my body, ran my hand through my hair, and hopped out of the bed. As I strolled to the washroom with hardly opened eyes, I felt this strong pull that made me want to curl up on the bed, basking in the warmth that only mornings like this could offer. I steeled my will against the tempting offer and allowed my feet to walk in the direction of the washroom.

My reflection in the mirror questioned the course of my life. Seriously, I had no idea. Like everybody else, I was relying on my fate for my future to unravel on its own; I was living life as it came my way. I took a shower to clear my indecisive thoughts, giving my mind much-needed calm.

Near my town, the Daffodils Art Museum was hosting an overnight art exhibition for charity. I had plans to visit the exhibition, so I dressed for the occasion and left for the venue.

The exhibition hall was exquisitely decorated. Soft music was playing in the background, and the mellow tune did not fail to ease the visitors' moods. The hall was not crowded. Only a few people were present, perhaps because it was not the weekend. More than sixty alluring paintings hung proudly on the walls of the venue, each captivating in its own way. The painting of a prince riding a chariot with his princess while people cheered and threw flowers particularly caught my attention. "This painting seems to have a bewitching charm," mesmerised a soft voice beside me. In a blink of an eye, I found myself staring at a beautiful young face covered in half by long, curly hair. The lilac-coloured knee-length dress she wore hugged her curves. A pearl necklace fell against the creamy expanse of her neck, and matching earrings dangled from her ears. Apart from the black kohl lining her eyes, no trace of makeup could be seen on her face. The stone on her bindi shone brightly, reflecting the light of the crystals in the chandelier that was proudly hanging from the ceiling right above us. Her brown orbs seemed to hide millions of secrets behind their luring perfection. She tucked a few strands of her messy curly hair behind her right ear as if my stare made her uncomfortable.

I shifted my gaze reluctantly back to the painting. "It does," I said, agreeing with her. As if it were all she wanted—for someone to agree with her—she turned back and walked away without sparing another word or a glance my way. Even after she left, her scent seemed to evade my senses, the strong smell of patchouli oil never fading away.

My thoughts were running wild. She was a nobody to me; she came out of nowhere; she went away like the wind; and still, her scent stayed imprinted in my senses. Somehow, it felt special. Unique, to be specific. The sun had gone down, immersing the world in darkness. I headed home, listening to the chirping of crickets. The moon shone brightly in the sky, bathing the way ahead with its pristine glow. A cold breeze flew past me, chilling my insides and freezing my bones. Never had a night been so beautiful, with the eerie calm adding to its haunting beauty. I looked around as my eyes searched for someone like me when I saw the same girl standing on the bridge, gazing into the river below. The aura surrounding her seemed to poke my curiosity; something about this stranger evoked a sense of mystery, and I found myself walking towards her, hoping to learn more. With every step I took, her face became clearer, as did the tears rolling down her cheeks that fell into the river, drop by drop.

I stood silently beside her, my eyes transfixed on the flowing water. "Have you ever felt the pain of separation?" she asked while her eyes were still gazing down at the ripples that formed below. She wiped her tears and continued, "Our fate is our worst enemy. Its cruelty knows no bounds. It even snatches our dearest one from us. Every moment we spend without that one person who is the centre of our universe is a curse. Suddenly, life feels like hell, the agony eating away at the shell of whatever is left of us." She paused; her eyes were now trained on me. "When you meet him on the journey of your life, tell him that I am waiting for him at the end of the earth." Her words didn't make any sense to me. Tears from her eyes kept streaming down her cheeks. We stood there in silence, none of us talking anymore. The silence itself seemed to speak volumes; it screamed, though inaudible, suffocating us.

In a flash, I found her hands surrounding my neck, strangling me. Her right hand held a knife, with which she stabbed me repeatedly on my shoulder. My helpless eyes found her watery orbs, silently begging for mercy. This time she jabbed hard, and instead of pulling it out, she pushed it down, further into my heart. My breath was laboured, each more difficult than the previous one. My eyes were trying hard to stay open; the vision of her watery eyes mixed with something mysterious and more alluring than ever. The bridge we were earlier standing on was now drowning in the crimson glory of my blood. The moon was smiling down at us, its soft light casting shadows around us. She bent down, taking my head in her lap, stroking my hair, and whispering as if in a trance. Sleep. Sleep. Sleep." I buried my head in her lap, pushing the world around us into some unknown abyss, and began to weep. My eyes were getting heavy, and I was gasping for air. My body was getting weak, and I was struggling to stay awake. With every passing moment, it was getting more and more difficult to see her face or hear her voice. She was whispering something into my ear. Her words were not clear to me, but they were my lullaby to fall into the abyss of unconsciousness. I looked at her face one last time in an attempt to decipher the puzzle behind her eyes and saw them filled with tears. The tears that rolled down her eyes fell onto my forehead, my last push to succumb to darkness.

I jolted awake on my bed, the shock successfully bringing me back to reality. I looked around, trying to find anything out of place or abnormal. I shifted my gaze to the ceiling. The ceiling fan above my head was going on at its fullest. Yet, I was sweating like I was put in an oven. It was as if a huge weight were placed on my chest—something so consuming, so soul-sucking. It was a foreign feeling, yet dangerously enticing. The art museum, the girl, her voice, the bridge, and everything else felt so real that it made me question my sanity. Was I going insane? Or does this convey any message to me? The dream vexed me to the point that I started getting Goosebumps every time I tried recalling it.

My phone started ringing. Leaving the bizarre dream to its fate, I sprang out of bed and walked to the side table where my phone was kept. Ben's name was flashing on the display, and it ceased ringing after a few seconds. I called him back, and he picked up my call in just one ring.

"Holla buddy, long time, no news?" came his voice from the other end, his melancholy tune deceiving the cheery words he used.

"Hi pal, I was a bit busy with work," I replied softly, rubbing my eyes to see the large analogue clock hanging above the bedpost as it struck 8.

"Are you free today? Let's meet and catch up. Stop by my resort when you are free."

It wasn't likely for him to call me out of the blue like this. I could warrant from his tone that he was desperate. Other than a few errands that I had to run in the morning, nothing was planned for the day. It was unlikely for anything to come up unannounced in the evening either. So, after a short contemplation of my own, I said, "Sure. I'll be there at six."

"See ya."

"See you," I said, hanging up.

I felt a throb at the base of my neck. One look in the mirror, and I was horrified. A small bruise adorned my neck, the sight making it impossible for me to move from the spot. Was my dream real? Just thinking about it sent chills down my spine. I peered out of the window, hoping to forget it all. As expected, nature worked its magic in scurrying me away from the dreaded dream.

Life is like a river; its course and flow are uniquely distinct, and it nourishes and vitalizes everything on its way. It's fascinating, the ebbs -- refreshing and awakening -- and the floods and droughts -- symbolising good and bad aspects of life. If a river is a blessing, so is life. Though unnerving and unpredictable, it is a blessing nonetheless.

Across the road in front of my house, there's a small pond. A few children were out there fishing, waiting around with bait.

A while later, I was waiting in my car for the signal to turn green. I saw an old man trying to cross the road. Parking my car sideways, I exited the comfort of the air conditioning and helped him cross the road. The smile he gave me in return was enough to brighten my remaining day.

Life, no matter which century we live in or what comforts we have, will always have ups and downs. That is how it works. Appreciating and acknowledging even the smallest fortunes will lead us a long way. Happiness can thus be found in everything, in every second.

On my way to the resort, I stopped by a cake shop. I saw a child crying for candy while the staff stood there, sending weird glances at his father. I took my order and left the building. Even when I was starting my car, the child didn't stop crying, and neither did his father relent to his wish.

When the sun was below the horizon, I saw a surprise greet me with a broad smile and bright eyes. It was my first encounter with Max, Ben's dog.

Max was a Labrador puppy that Ben started sheltering some time back. Ben had found Max in some abandoned place, and he was lucky enough to be rescued by Ben. He had a brown coat and captivating golden-honey eyes. His coat was incredibly soft and well-groomed. As soon as he saw me, he came running towards me and greeted me. He started wagging his tail to express his happiness and love, and he warmly welcomed me.

Ben accompanied me to the table and sat opposite me. He filled our glasses with wine and placed a plate of hot chips on the table for us to munch on, while the dog rested near the seat he was about to take. A feeble symphony was playing in the background. His hands were shivering as he poured the wine. He sat down and immediately sipped on the wine to steady his shaky hand while his other hand caressed the dog's fur. His eyes were broody; something untold was swirling behind them. It felt as if he wanted to tell me something but was unable to. So, I decided to give him a start by breaking the ice between us.

"So, who's this?" I asked, nodding my head towards the dog, whose gaze was now fixed on me.

Ben jolted in his seat as if my question had woken him from some unknown trance. "Oh? Him? He's my best buddy. Without him, darkness would've won over me long ago." He said, his hand still running through the dog's fur.

"But with him here, we won't be able to talk freely. He'd want me to pet him constantly." Ben said, standing up from his seat and pulling Max's leash.

"Ah… attention seeker." I murmured, more to myself.

Ben went away with Max for a few minutes and came back alone. Taking his seat again, he began to nurse his wine glass once again, humming and nodding to my words.

A little into our conversation, he asked, "Ashiq, may I ask you something serious?"

"Yeah. "What's with the heads up?"

"What is your concept of love?"

I felt a grin forming on my face as I answered, "We all are born to love and to experience the true form of love. Sooner or later, all of us will feel loved. Love will play a crucial role in all of our lives."

"True," his sound was so low that I had to strain my ears to hear it. He leaned back in his chair and looked up at the sky.

"Isn't it beautiful?" he asked.

"You mean the sky? Yes, the night is just beautiful, and it seems like someone sprinkled glitter all over it. We are like the moon, always boasting our brighter side but not the darker." I said and looked over to him to find his eyes trained on me.

His eyes met mine, never looking away, as he asked, "There are 365 days in a year. Out of all these days, why did we choose to meet today, January 20th?"

"Is there anything special today?" I asked as I leaned back on the chair, crossing my legs.

"Yes. Life is unpredictable, and I still can't believe something like this has happened to me. A few years ago, on this very same day, fate mocked my life and changed it upside down."

I kept listening, not understanding where this conversation was heading as he continued, "In my dreams, I always see two paths. The path to my right is a well-laid one that leads to a glorious life. The path to my left is a bumpy one with an unknown destination and a faint glow of light leading my way. If you were standing in my place, which path would you choose? The path to my right guarantees me all the success and happiness in the world. But I wish to trudge on with the other one. The one which leads me nowhere, the one which promises nothing but hardships."

"But why Ben? All of us wish to be happy and successful one day. When you are so sure of it, why does the unknown path of hardship entice you?" His words made no sense to me. Yet I knew if I were in his position, I would choose the path to happiness over the other, which could possibly land me in the middle of nowhere.

"Every day I keep convincing myself to move away from my haunted dreams, but now I've given up hope. I can't escape my reality." His words held contempt, and the sorrow in them frightened me.

"Reality?" I asked in a rough tone. My own voice felt foreign to me.

By then, Ben was breathing heavily.

Fat tears were rolling down his cheeks. Suddenly, he took hold of my hands and brawled, "Ashiq, I committed a homicide." His eyes held so much pain and guilt that it pierced my heart. The anger, sorrow, and dejection in his eyes were so deeply rooted in his heart. I searched for a silver line of hope in them, which unfortunately was answered with coldness and sorrow. "I killed an innocent girl."

PART 1

Love is strange. We just can't decide its course. Nobody can foresee when, where, or how it will come into your life. Every love story happens on its own; its pace is different from others, and its flow is unique. It connects hearts immediately, leaving us out of choices; the pull of that bond is beyond our control; it takes a fine moment to realise that the force is built over months and sometimes years. No matter how much we take pride in being in control of our minds, when it comes to this particular emotion, the heart always gets the upper hand. When the heart rivals the mind, emotions fight reason, and thoughts confront actions, all we can do is look on and watch the struggle from afar. In an instant, a stranger becomes the centre of one's world. They become the sole reason for people to live, sometimes to die and kill, and they become their only goal in life. Empires were built and felled for the very same emotion. Clans have been united, friends have become rivals, and cities have been burned to the ground. Monuments were erected, and sculptures were bathed in blood. The thought of losing them physically hurts and makes it difficult even to breathe. Once in love, life suddenly becomes intriguing. So simple, yet complex beyond our comprehension. A smile or an innocent touch can brighten up our whole world; even a moment of separation will seem like hours in the deepest pits of hell.

Ben's thoughts were scattered as he strolled down the deserted road to his home. The day was slightly cloudy and young. Bright red flowers carpeted his path, making him throw his head back. Gulmohar trees lined the sidewalk, offering their shadows to anyone who walked by. They seemed to touch the sky; flames of red licked the heavens, and the beauty of it was hauntingly warm. He loved it—the morning sun, the warmth that only these shadows could extend, the happy chirps of the birds, and the soft trudge of his. The warm, mushy feelings that tickled him made lone strolls like this one of his favourites.

The blast of loud pop music from his phone made him stop in his tracks. Irritated, he pulled the phone from his pocket to see the word "Mom" flashing on the screen. Somehow, a smile made its way to his face, his lips curling at the sides. No matter which daydreams he was woken up from if it was for his mom, he didn't mind. He pressed the answer button, making a mental note to change the annoying ringtone on his phone later. As soon as the call connected, a feminine, not-so-soft voice shouted from the other end.

"Where are you? When are you getting back?" Her tone may come off as audacious to others, for the concern and worry etched in it were only meant for him to understand.

"Mom, why do you worry so much? I am on my way. Will be there soon." His voice conveyed a gentle assurance that only he could gift his mother.

"If not me, who else will worry for you? The weather forecast said it might rain today. Don't you dare step into my home, all drenched! Mark my words, boy, if you fall sick, it's all on you. I won't spare a glance towards your sickly self." She shot back.

Laughter bubbled in him as he listened to her empty threats. He knew it would hurt her more if he fell sick. Threats like these? He received them on a daily basis. Yet she would do everything to contradict her words.

"Aye, aye, Captain. I heard you loud and clear. I'll be home before it starts raining, okay?" He smiled, hearing her sigh.

"You better," he heard her say. The line went off as he smiled to himself.

As if on cue, it started pouring, the heavens giving into the earth's cry for elixir. He jogged towards the parking lot of a nearby house, which was a few blocks away from his own abode, in hopes to protect himself from the wrath of clouds.

He was patting himself dry when a sweet voice chimed in. "Hi, Ben!"

He turned towards the not-so-familiar voice to see a familiar face smiling at him.

"Hi, Apoorva." He greeted her back in a constricted voice. His breaths were ragged, and his heartbeat was abnormally fast because of the short jog he took.

Unconsciously, his eyes ran over her, noticing every detail that, until now, had never captured his attention. Brown orbs filled with apprehension, hope, delight, and much more stared back. The brightness and twinkle that he saw in them made him question his own sanity. Her black mane fell back over her shoulders, and a few strands stuck to her rosy cheeks. As if by habit, her long, slender fingers brushed the rogue strands back, pinning them behind her ears. Even then, her eyes never left his as she grinned at him like a Cheshire cat. The moment felt ethereal to him. Time stopped, and the world around him stilled. Her eyes seemed to stop him in his tracks, leaving him unable to move or speak. She looked so beautiful and breathtaking, like a rare flower, so delicate and precious. So many unanswered questions swirled in his mind, mocking his trans fixture.

"Oh!!! Now we understand. This is why you felt so bored with us."

Ben jolted back to reality at the teasing voice of one of Apoorva's friends. One of the girls was pointing at him, while two others looked on curiously.

"Errm…ah... I was enjoying the rain. Yeah. I was just enjoying the rain." She quoted the word 'just' with her hands.

Apoorva's response was strange. She seemed overwhelmed by the whole situation. Her eyes nervously darted from him to her friends. She started swaying from side to side as she shifted her weight from one foot to another with her hands tied behind her back. Her words sounded more like lame excuses, which her friends seemed to catch on to. The awkward nervousness rolled off her in waves, which made him strangely uncomfortable. He said nothing as they stared ahead. Her friends kept their distance, but he could feel their eyes on him as a meaningful silence hung between them. He knew that they were just watching out for her. He had seen the four musketeers often in the past backing each other like rocks as they continued to celebrate their youth. Those were the mere observations of an onlooker. Things were changing as he struggled to make out the trail of his thoughts. He realised this with excitement and apprehension as his role changed from that of an onlooker to that of an admirer.

Grey clouds traversed the sky. Birds started singing, and the refreshing scent of petrichor teased their nostrils. After a slow drizzle that seemed to last forever, Ben bid goodbye to Apoorva and weaved his way back home.

Apoorva watched his retreating back until he was no longer in her sight. She turned back to leave to meet her friends' challenging gazes. Apoorva, Sminu, Emma, and Niha were friends since their diaper days. They were more like sisters than friends. The girls were as thick as thieves, practically glued to each other.

Good friends are like hidden treasures. Friendship extends the meaning of brotherhood beyond ties of blood. Trust and honesty became the common ground on which this beautiful relationship was built. Losing a good friend is like losing one's own soul. Finding one good friend can prove to be difficult. All we can do is hold on to the good ones that we got by chance. She never hid anything from her friends. All her secrets were her friends' too. To them, she was an open book. Her admiration for Ben was something that she never shared with them. She liked Ben, but she never thought about the 'like' she had for him enough to discuss it with her friends. Today seemed to change something. Ben was different; his gaze on her was different. He seemed to gaze at her with admiration and hope, unlike their previous encounters, when his smiles friend-zoned her. She looked around, trying to find a way to escape their interrogation.

"You are not taking another step until you clearly answer all our questions." Niha threatened as she popped a peanut into her mouth.

"What questions? Ask away. You know you can ask me anything. I never kept secrets from you guys." She shot back, trying to play it cool.

"Ah haa... That's what we thought. That you never keep secrets from us. But seeing you blush like a tomato in front of a guy who just passed by tells us that you haven't been telling us everything all along. Right, Sminu?" Emma asked, trying to get Sminu talking.

"He's sooo handsome. What is his name? Can I have him?" Sminu asked, totally mesmerised.

"His name is Benedict. And no. You can't have him." She shouted back. Her voice went up an octave in her effort to stop Sminu from getting her hopes up.

"Why? Do you like him?" Sminu asked as her smile turned mischievous.

How big of a fool was she? She knew her friends like the back of her hand. Yet she gave so easily into Sminu's trap. She shifted her gaze to others, as they all wore the same smug expression.

"So..... do you like him or not? Tell us the truth, sweety. With that response of yours, I'd say that you blew your cover beyond repair." Niha mused.

That's it. She was busted. She could no longer keep it from them. She knew that.

"Tone it down a bit, will you? Yes, I like him." She admitted hesitantly.

"And?" Sminu asked as she prodded for more.

"And I've known him since childhood. Always a charming gentleman." She smiled at the end, remembering his sweet smiles and soft words.

"Charming gentleman, huh? Look at that smile of hers. Don't you think that she's a gone case?" Emma teased, making her smile wider.

"Apoorva?" A voice came from the house.

"Ma!!!!!" she shouted back as panic laced her voice.

"Where are you, child? Did you go out to play in the rain?" Her mom asked.

"No, Ma. I didn't. I am just watching it rain. I didn't get wet, I promise." She shouted back, relieved that her mom didn't hear any of their bickering.

"That's enough. Come, help me with something." She could hear the exhaustion in her voice.

"Coming." She shouted back and turned to her friends.

"Okay. Now, that's our cue to leave." Emma said.

"No, wait; stay. What are you girls rushing back to? Spend some more time here, with me." She insisted in hopes of making them stay longer.

"Hey Missy, we are not saying goodbye forever. I've got plans with family tonight. I can't afford to be late. That's why." Niha added.

"But..." She tried coming up with excuses.

"Appu, I think Niha's right. It looks like it's going to rain heavily today. So, it's better if we leave now." Emma suggested, successfully stopping her from saying any more.

Okay," she muttered, distress clear in her voice.

"Don't worry, Missy. We'll come back to see that charming gentleman again." Sminu laughed and ran as she lifted her hand to swat her.

"Fine. See you tomorrow." She shouted as her friends waved back.

She could hear her mom shouting from inside the house to help her clean the table. She walked through the garden, caressing the flowers and enjoying the cold breeze. She was about to lean down and smell the rose flower that she recently planted when her mom shouted, "Appuuu…" She stood up, startled by the scream. Now, if she didn't rush back home, her mom would personally come out and haul her ass to the kitchen. She skipped forward, hoping to keep the annoyance away from her face. The sky seemed so dark today that she thought it would keep raining. She wanted to stay outside, soak in the rain, and let the sweet scent of petrichor enter her nostrils. But her mom seemed to smell her intentions from miles away. Maybe if she made no sound and walked past the dining hall without making a sound, she could escape from the chores. So, she danced her way into the drawing room, whistling a mellow tune and caressing the carnations that smiled at her brightly from the flower vase, and came to an abrupt halt near the dining hall entrance. From there, she trod slowly without making a noise, being extra cautious about every step she took. Just when she was about to succeed in her mission, came her mom's yell: "Help me clean the table, Apoorva. You can't fool me, baby." Apoorva peeked into the dining hall to see her mother's back turned towards her. She was picking up the dirty dishes and leftover food from the table. How she managed to catch her before she passed the dining room will always remain a mystery to her. Nonetheless, if she was caught in the act, she might as well help her mom with cleaning. So she skipped into the dining room, singing, Sure, mom."

"How are your friends? Were they comfortable here?" her mom asked.

"Yes, they are all good, and they felt at home here."

"Did you see her room? It's all messed up because of her friends," Annie shouted.

Annie was Apoorva's younger sister and her major rival at home. Not a day went by without them pulling each other's hair. Even then, they loved each other to bits. Both of them knew that if anything were to happen to the other, life would come to a halt for them too.

"Don't ever speak like that about my friends," Apoorva shouted. As usual, her hands went to Annie's hair, making her shriek.

"Mom, she is pulling my hair." "It's hurting," Annie cried.

"Will you stop? You're both grownups. Behave properly. If your father gets a whiff of your quarrels, he'll be worried. He loves you both too much to see you quarrelling with each other."

Apoorva and Annie were not short of anything in life from their childhood on, thanks to their dad. He loved them unconditionally, and the girls knew that he'd do anything to make their lives comfortable. The one thing he hated the most was their quarrels. And the girls didn't want to get on their dad's bad side. A truce was what they would prefer rather than letting their dad get a hint of their daily drama.

"Sorry mom, don't say anything to papa. Sorry, Appu." Annie was quick to apologise. Their fights never lasted beyond a few minutes, thanks to their parents. Her family was the best, and her parents were everything any girl could ever wish for. Her sister was a royal pain in the ass most of the time, yet Apoorva knew that she wouldn't trade her for the whole world.

"Why are you so late? Have you seen the time? At least, you could've taken an umbrella with you. It would've stopped me from worrying so much. Ben's mother shouted from the entrance of his house. He smiled, her words falling on deaf ears. He knew that his mom could never think past those smiles of his. Just as he was about to throw a cheesy comment her way, she raised her hand, signalling a big no. His mouth closed, turning into what he thought was an adoringly cute pout.

"I don't want to hear your stupid excuses or see that monkey face of yours. Get fresh first and come down. No more excuses." His pout morphed into a look of pure embarrassment, the hilariousness of which made his dad keep both his hands on his mouth to stop himself from laughing out loud. Ben ran upstairs, not wanting to hear more from his mom. His ego was already badly hurt; he didn't want to kill it with his mom's scathing words.

A few minutes later, he was climbing down the stairs, clean and fresh in his favourite sweatshirt and joggers, looking every bit like the "Greek god" his fan girls called him to be.

He wanted to prove a point to his mom. Maybe she was unaware of the popularity he had at school because of his amazing good looks. So, today, he took special care to keep his hair messy, which was a swoon-worthy factor for many. His mom was sitting on the sofa, opposite his dad, waiting for him to join them. The smell of freshly brewed coffee teased his nostrils, making him feel at home like never before. As his mom poured the coffee from the jug into the cups, he made it a point to stand at a 2-foot distance from her, just so she would notice his good looks. Once done, she gave a cup to his father, looked at him, and said, "Here's your coffee, sir." She took one cup into her hand, and took a sip, savouring the beverage. Ben was annoyed beyond limits. Didn't she notice how good he looked? If she didn't, he was going to make her. So, he cleared his throat to garner attention, which it clearly did. His dad was now looking at him with narrowed eyes, and his mom had her eyebrows raised at him. "So... how do I look?" he asked, wiggling his eyebrows at his mom. Those raised eyebrows went down a bit as she took another sip from her coffee. "You look every bit like the monkey that you were from the time I gave birth to you." She said that and went back to sipping her coffee. His dad was trying hard to keep a straight face, from what he could tell. His shoulders slouched as he walked to the sofa to sit near his father, grabbing his coffee cup from the tray.

"So, how was your day, son?" Ben's dad asked, hoping to save him from the embarrassment.

"I went to get this book," he gestured with his right hand and read, "You can heal your life by Louis L. Hay. The book is based on self-healing and focuses on mental and physical health. I loved it so much that I got it issued. Everyone must read this," suggested Ben.

"Yes, you should read more of these books; they will have a huge impact on your character formation," his father told him.

"Also, dad, while on the way back home, I saw a pregnant lady. She had a big bump and was having real difficulty in walking," he said, even the mental picture of her giving him chills.

His mom, who had only been focused on her coffee until then, placed the cup on the tray and said, "Ben, this is normal. Every woman goes through this phase. I also experienced this at the time of your birth. You feel numb, dizzy, and moody, and you face hormonal imbalances all the time. Sometimes you like something while, at the next moment, you begin to hate it. Women have to go through a lot in their lives. Every person should be given equal opportunities to study, work, get a job, and build a career of their choice, irrespective of their gender. You must ensure every time that no person, especially a female, faces gender bias in your presence. You must always raise your voice against all the wrong deeds," she stated, her eyes speaking volumes.

"I know, mom." Ben replied. "And I will never do that consciously. Now, please pass me the snacks." He said, hoping not to pout too much. What if she made the monkey reference again? He wouldn't be able to take that blow again.

As his mom extended the snack plate towards him, his dad butted in, "Me and Ben are going on a walk after the coffee. And you, my dear wife," he said, looking at Ben's mom, "are not invited."

Ben's mom shook her head, sporting a smile on her face. She stood up, gathered the cups and plates in a tray, and walked into the kitchen, leaving Ben and his dad to themselves.

After putting on their shoes and jackets, they walked out, welcoming the hustle and bustle of the road with lowered voices.

"Mom's such a bully, Dad. Still, you say that she's the one. How do you keep up with her? Didn't you have any other option?" Ben asked, breaking the silence that stretched between them.

His dad smiled, surprising Ben. "We all have numerous options, Ben. All we have to do is choose right. And I strongly believe that I chose right. I made no mistake. And never in the last 20 years did I think otherwise. I have no regrets or complaints about the woman she is."

They strolled into the nearby park, finding a bench under the shadow of a mango tree.

"She was there with me at every step I took, even when I had doubts about myself. She never doubted me or blamed me for my failures. With every step I took, I had her by my side, never leaving me to paddle alone. When we had you, she had a career break of about 5 years. She stayed home, tending to you alone, never uttering a word of complaint or annoyance. For all we knew, it could as well be the end of her career. Who will hire her after such a lengthy break? I know I wouldn't. Still, she gave everything she had for you, wholeheartedly. Love is not always about hugs and kisses, as you see in movies or on social media these days. There's more to love than that. And your mom, if you ask me, is the very definition of love and self-sacrifice. Sitting in the house tending to a toddler without having daily social interactions with your peers every day for five years seems like a herculean task to me. If I were her, I would've at least quarrelled with myself for that. I hope now you understand why your mother is my only choice. I hope this makes you realise why your mother should always be a priority for you, Ben."

"I understand, dad." Ben nodded his head, staring at the sky.

"But I have to admit that her insults are scathing." Ben's dad said, evoking a burst of loud laughter from the duo.

"So, is there anything else that I can help you with? I have an intuition that something else is bothering you." His dad prodded, making Ben look at his dad surprisingly.

"No, let me change that a bit." His dad said "Your mother had an intuition that something was bothering you. And she asked me to talk to you."

Ben smiled, shaking his head gently. His mom was a gem in every sense. He was just too dumb to realise it so late.

"I have, dad. I have this fear that I won't get admission to my favourite course. I don't think I can study anything else. What should I do?" Ben let out a sigh, feeling the comfort of a heavy weight being lifted off his chest.

"Son, you are scared of an admission? Believe me, these are not the biggest problems that you face in life. This is just a sample. Life will throw a lot more at your way of life. If you lose your footing now, you'll never even have a chance to stand again. So be brave and believe in yourself. Your consistency, efforts, and hard work will surely pay off one day."

Ben was now a lot calmer. He now had the motivation and time to work towards his goal.

As they were talking, his dad got a call from his friends. He attended the call and turned back to Ben.

"Son, go home and tell your mom that you were cold and had to return. I have to meet a friend of mine for something important. Please tell her that I'm still at the park and will return after some time."

Ben knew his dad. Something important meant he was going to his friends' for a couple of drinks. His mom was not a fan of his dad's drinking, and if she knew, they'd quarrel over it for at least two days.

And Ben was certainly not looking forward to that. But he couldn't help but pull his leg a bit.

"Something important, huh? If I told her that you were out for a drink, she'd definitely reward me for my honesty by getting me anything I wanted. But, before that, I wanted to know what you'd be offering me for my silence. What would you offer me, dad, for not breathing a word to mom?" he asked, feeling smug.

His dad's widened eyes met his as the man gulped. He knew what would happen if his wife got a whiff of his escapades with his friends. Now, he had to make sure that Ben would stay silent about it too. He looked around and saw an ice cream van.

"Ice cream?" he asked, looking at his son, who looked no less than a devil then.

"Ice cream? Cheee…. Dad, what am I? 5?" he asked, his face full of disgust. "Mom will gift me a pair of Nikes if I rat you out." Offer me something better, and I shall keep my silence." Ben bargained, raising an eyebrow at his dad.

"How about the latest G-Shock watch that you were showing me?" dad asked, making Ben grin.

"Perfect. Now you can go do that something important with your friends, and I shall cover up for you at home." Ben said, air-quoting 'something important'. He hugged his dad and jogged back home, letting his father stand there astounded.

While he was jogging back home, he couldn't help but smile non-stop like a lunatic. This was something he didn't expect, and he knew that he was going to make the most of the opportunity. That is why he didn't see Apoorva coming his way, fully engrossed in her own thoughts. All he could register was a crash and someone falling on the floor.

Apoorva was strolling along the sidewalk, enjoying the cold rush of night air. The night sky was clear, and there was no sign of rain anytime soon. She was awestruck by the picturesque image the alley painted when someone rushed over and hit his head with hers. The unexpected force pulled her down, and she fell back with a yell. She looked up, planning to give her offender an earful. Just then, Ben squatted down near her, an apologetic look on his face.

"Aww... My head... It hurts." she complained, keeping her hand on her forehead.

"I'm sorry. So sorry. I didn't see you. Come on. Let me help you." He said it apologetically and extended his hand to pull her up.

"Sorry? What sorry?" She yelled, standing tall on her own and dusting herself, refusing the olive branch he extended.

Ben moved closer to her to see her forehead swelling. He caressed the swelling with his fingers, hoping to lessen her pain. Her forehead just came up to his chest, making him hover over her. The sweetness of her vanilla-scented shampoo teased his nostrils, making his inhales more fervent.

"I am really sorry. I didn't mean to knock you down. I hope you aren't hurt." His voice held true remorse over what happened. He pulled out a chocolate from the back pocket of his jeans and extended it towards her as a token of remorse. Apoorva's face lit up upon seeing the chocolate, and she excitedly reached out to take it in her hands like a kid.

"It's okay. I am alright. But where are you rushing to?" She asked as she straightened her clothes.

"Home. And where are you headed to?" Ben asked.

"Me too. Let's walk together." She suggested, directing her puppy dog eyes towards him.

At that moment, he felt the spark that was ignited between them. He saw the gleam in her eyes and its transformation from innocent adoration to tender love. Her lips mirrored the delicacy of rose petals. Her rosy cheeks glowed under the light rays of the sun. They walked forward, falling into sync with each other. Ben's arms rubbed against Apoorva's, sending a shockwave of chill down his spine. His heart skipped a beat at the contact as he pushed his hands further into the pockets of his jeans. The path seemed unending, never putting a stop to their stroll. She changed his life like no other. They hadn't parted yet, but all he could think of was the next time he would meet her.

25

It wasn't midst the crowd

Or a choice she made.

She didn't pick him from the rest

For she never thought of anyone else.

It was in the air she breathes

With every breath she took,

It was in the clouds above

From where he'd descent,

She waited along

For him so very long.

| **PART 2**

Another day was approaching its end. The sun was setting, painting the sky red with its dwindling rays. Birds were chirping loudly as they frantically flew away from the day's hard work to the comfort of their nests. Twilight retreated, its bright hue vanishing into thin air, like a picture painted on a canvas—leaving it for the moon to take over. A few stars were scattered by the moon, capturing my heart as my mind pondered over ideas, back and forth. I rolled my pen between my fingers, hoping to continue writing anything that I could pour into these blank pages without having to think twice... No matter how hard I tried, writing further seemed no less than a herculean task. I stretched lazily like a feline, threw my head back, and jiggled my shoulders, hoping to relieve the ache in my muscles. Capping the pen, I kept it inside my diary and pushed myself up from the chair, hearing its screech on the floor. Walking onto the balcony, I felt the cool air hit my face as an odd sense of pensiveness took over. I paced around, enjoying the chilly weather, my mind far from the composure my posture projected. The distinct sound of my ringtone could be heard. Ignoring it, I stared ahead.

"Boy, are you deaf? Your phone's been ringing for so long. It's April. Come down and answer it." I heard my mom shout. The incessant ringing might have ticked her off.

"Coming, mom," I yelled back, my mind nowhere near letting go of the precious moment it was savouring.

I pulled out a cigarette from my pocket, lit it, and took a few deep puffs. The smoke entered my entire being, caressing my insides and intoxicating my nerves with its toxic haze.

Standing there, staring into the night, I felt like I was frozen in time. I stood there, light years away from the world, where watches ticked away relentlessly. My eyes fixed on nothing, my brain taking its time off. It felt good, calming in a sense. Isn't it odd that time is alike for all, rich or poor, old or young? Yet we live with different ideas of time. An eternity for me must feel like a moment for somebody else. It waits for none; no barrier limits its flow. And yet we hope for it to stand still for a second, give us a moment, run back a little, and come up with a manual. Every moment we have spent is a memory. Like our footsteps, which are washed away into the sea by waves, time washes away time, which is too precious to let go without a thought, be it good or bad. I sometimes wish to possess a time machine so that I can go back to my past, erase some memories, undo some mistakes, and replace them with something fond. I've read somewhere: "Blessed are the forgetful". But I doubt if you have to be forgetful when you are among those who find true love. It is an emotion that is beyond what words can express or actions can prove. Those efforts and commitments we put in are all nurtured with care. Like friendship, love too flourishes on trust, loyalty, understanding, and support. When in love, perfection becomes unreal. Imperfections, for once, give people the much-needed assurance their dear ones are real, not gods.

A few raindrops fell on my face, waking me from my immersive thoughts. I stood there, waiting for more to fall. When Ben told me his story, I was really confused. We all have skeletons in our closets, waiting to break out. Confessing those to someone voluntarily takes a lot of courage. For Ben to share his story with me, he must have thought a lot. So many unanswered questions haunted my conscience, making my thoughts run wild. What made him confide in me? It felt as if, slowly, I was becoming his confidant. The lingering thoughts were not letting go of me. How did a story so odd find its way to me? I do not know. The weight of it has now become mine to bear too. I was stuck in a never-ending loop, forming an unruly maze in my head. In a night, life turned upside down as peace traded places with chaos. Unrest accompanied me wherever I went, making it difficult to even breathe. Sorrow, fear, and concern took hold of my heart in a vile grip, leaving me defenceless and vulnerable.

"Counting stars?" A voice came, bursting the bubble of my thoughts and saving me from the dangerous territory my thoughts were treading. I turned around and chuckled at the playful comment. It was Sarah, my neighbour, who lived next to my house in the lane. She was the happy-go-lucky kind, who could light up even the dimmest of rooms. She had this weird playfulness in her that would make us forget all our worries once she started talking.

"Why? Planning to join me?" I shot back, returning her smile.

"Not if it's as boring as you."

"You wound me, lady," I said, placing a hand over my heart.

"I try." Sarcasm dripped down her words, making me smile wider.

"And, you are here for?" I asked, raising my eyebrows questioningly.

"Duh!!! Smooth. Just tell me that you can't stand my presence anymore. I am getting out of your hair soon. I came to take my clothes." She replied, making me laugh out loud.

"I didn't say that," I said, raising my hands in mock surrender. "Well, how's life?" I asked, trying to make small talk. I desperately needed a distraction from everything that hounded me, and she somehow seemed to ease my mind with her sarcastic comments.

"Life's good, I guess." She said, nodding her head. "What about you?" She asked.

"Life's life," I said, not knowing the exact answer.

"That's some life." She mused. "By the way, are you deaf or something? Your mom has been yelling for an hour or so. Go and have something." she said, reminding me of my needs.

"You heard that?" I asked, embarrassed. The whole neighbourhood might have heard my mom.

"Not only me." She pointed around. "You better go and have something. Or else, she might start yelling again." She said, waving her hands at me, leaving me alone to ponder over my thoughts.

My days were normal until I met Ben. Hearing him pour his heart out, it is as if life has taken on another dimension, something beyond my conception, I was unable to differentiate dreams from reality. I couldn't help but keep a journal so that I could refer to it whenever the dilemma presented itself before me. It has now become a habit I can't get rid of since storing memories in their purest and maiden form seems more important than ever. No matter how hard I tried, some moments refused to stay trapped within the pages of memories. Living them seemed enough—the experience was more beautiful than the grey nostalgia those pages offered. I began to savour every moment as if there were no tomorrow, hoping for life to break me into pieces with every passing second. It is a package of thrills and scares rolled into one. The thrill of life, to do everything that seemed difficult once, scared for the loss that I expect to wait for me at the end of the tunnel. Life, in short, as I told Sarah, has been life. No other words could describe it better.

I went downstairs and took my phone. 15 missed calls from April She'd have my head for ignoring her calls. I called back, hoping to tame the lioness. In half a ring, the call got connected, and a shriek came from the other end. "Where were you? I've been calling you for the past 2 hours. Why didn't you answer?"

"Well, madam, I was pondering over my thoughts," I said, smiling at my reflection in the mirror.

"Will you stop with your poetic profanities? I am a human being whose IQ is much below yours. Cut me some slack, genius." She replied sarcastically. I couldn't help but laugh at her choice of words.

"Seriously, I didn't hear the ring. I was somewhere deep." I said, sounding more serious.

"Let me guess, you were thinking about Ben and that weird conversation that you had with him. Am I right?" She asked, sounding proud.

"Ha!!! Who's the genius now?" I asked, happy that she got it right without having to explain it.

I am surprised and proud every time she gets my emotions right. I don't know how I ever got a chance to meet a girl like her. She knows me like the back of her hand and understands me without many words. A slight change in my tone, a glance, or a simple touch is more than enough for her to understand me, no matter how trivial those gestures may seem to others.

"Don't think too much. Get your mind off the gutter and pack your bags. It is my brother's wedding in a few days, and you are there, thinking over something sad. We are all waiting for your arrival; remember that." She said both, calming and admonishing me at once.

"I'll be there on time, princess," I said as a full-blown smile made its way to my face at the thought of seeing her.

"I wanted to ask you this earlier but was put off until the end. It's your brother's Remembrance Day, right? I honestly wanted to be there, but with this marriage preparation, I just couldn't. I am sorry." She spoke, her tone hitting its lowest octave.

"Hey, hey, it's okay. Your brother's wedding is more important than anything else. And I know that you can't bail out on it. I am so glad to have someone like you by my side. It is perfectly fine; they need you there. Now off you go. Because by the time I am there, I need your full attention on me. See you soon, love." I said, meaning every word I uttered.

"See you and love you too," she said, hanging up the call.

I walked to the drawing room and pulled a cabinet drawer open. It was full of albums, filled with memories of our happy times. I took an album out and flipped through the photos. Some were mine; some were Chiku's; and then, some had my mom and dad smiling brightly. I looked at every picture. We were all happy. We all had smiles on our faces. We looked content. Chiku's condition would have been a killjoy to many, but it never dimmed our happiness, not even by a bit. We considered it a privilege that we got to look after him. With him, my mom's smiles never died. It stayed in its place, making us all smile in its wake. Mom always told me that God chose us as Chiku's family because he could see the goodness in our hearts. He knew that we would take care of him, no matter what hardships came our way. We looked after him like the treasure he was, trying to make him happy with every action of ours. Life was so beautiful back then. Our small family was complete. Every waking minute of our lives went by devoid of any regrets. Our moments with each other were never less than any celebration, and we never let go of the chances that were meant to be celebrated. Life was so colourful, and love seemed to be abundant. Never have I ever imagined that I'd stand at this point in life, thinking about him in the past. Whenever I thought of the future, it was never mine alone; it was his too. I saw him walking with me through our lives, both of us welcoming and embracing the different seasons of life with changes in our own selves. He brought tears to my eyes every time I thought about him. Not a day went by without a memory of his. It's been eight years since he left this world. He was suffering from 'cerebral palsy', a condition caused by injury to the parts of the brain that control our ability to use our muscles and bodies. It can occur before birth, sometimes during childbirth, or soon after birth. My brother was a CP child from the womb itself. He was completely bedridden and couldn't move a muscle without help. He had round black eyes, a cute button nose, chubby cheeks, short brown hair, and long, slender fingers.

My father always believed that my brother was a genius. He told me that Chiku would score better than me if he ever had a chance to go to school. He was not wrong. Chiku was a genius, and if not for that demented sickness, he would have conquered great heights. My mother deserved the credit for his brilliance. Despite him being a CP child, my mom never gave up on him and his studies. She didn't care if he never left his bed or conquered the world. She wanted him to learn new things and explore the world from within the boundaries of our house. Despite being chained to the bed for a lifetime, he never cursed his fate and never forgot to smile. When we were kids, I used to run to his room to escape my mom's wrath. I would sit on his bed, clutching his hand tightly, while mom scolded me. He always helped me cope with my troublesome self. Whenever I wanted to share something or needed a shoulder to cry on, he was there. My joys and sorrows were his, and his were mine. He knew me like no one else. Our interactions were different from those of normal brothers, for he was more of a friend to me. A friend who knew me better than myself.

I used to take him for evening walks. He would sit in his special wheelchair, enjoying the breeze and watching others pass by, while I pushed him from behind. The memories of those walks are priceless treasures that I desperately wish to relive. When he was alive, I spent every waking moment with him. We watched TV together, had food together, and studied together. We did nothing apart, and that made our bond even stronger.

When he laughed, it lit up my whole world, and when he cried, my heart ripped with every tear he shed. Whenever I went out, he waved and blew kisses at me. Therapies were a part of his routine, though they were never effective. Fond memories clutched my heart in an unforgivable grip, making my eyes water.

My grandmother used to talk a lot about Chiku's condition and the difficulties my parents faced in his upbringing. I've read stories about people killing their kids owing to their disabilities, but my parents fought against all odds and did everything they could for Chiku. Whenever I think of people who harm children just because they are disabled, I feel pity. How can anyone kill such innocent beings? It's not their fault that they are differently abled. If treated with proper

love, care, and affection, I know that they will give you much more in
return.

I checked my watch as it struck noon. I was waiting in the domestic terminal of Trivandrum International Airport to take a flight to Mumbai to attend April's brother, Joye's, wedding. My cell phone vibrated in my pocket as April's name flashed on the screen.

"Did you reach the airport?" As soon as the call was connected, April's cheerful voice came through.

"Yup. I'm about to board." I said. As if on cue, an announcement came, calling for passengers to board the flight.

"When will you reach here?" she asked, her voice trembling with excitement.

"It's a non-stop flight. I may reach there in two hours, I guess," I answered, nodding to the hostess who greeted me at the entrance.

"Ok. Roshan will pick you up from the airport. I have texted you his contact information. Call him once you get off the flight."

"Yeah. Meet you soon, babe." I said, my excitement getting the best of me.

"Take care," she said, hanging up.

April is everything that I could have ever asked for in a partner. With her, it was never about expensive dinners or vacations, she never made me doubt my worth. No matter which ditch I fell into, she always stood by me and supported me. It is the connection and compassion we share that I'm eternally grateful for; I couldn't have asked for more.

I looked out, watching the clouds floating like cotton balls. The beautiful view seemed to capture me, making it impossible to tear my eyes from it. A sense of calm invaded my senses, making me forget about my surroundings. A toddler's high-pitched wails pulled me out of my trance. I looked around, trying to find the source, and found a young mother trying hard to make the child stop. I started making funny faces at the child, effectively stopping his wails as he looked at me with curiosity. I moved my hands around and rolled my eyes, making him smile. His mother seemed to relax a bit, as she turned and gave me a nod of gratitude.

With every passing second, excitement was bubbling up in me at the thought of seeing April. Time seemed to stretch on forever, and when the announcement for landing came, I was more interested in getting out than buckling up. I got off the flight and passed all the customary security checks. As I walked out, I remembered that it was her cousin who was supposed to pick me up, not her. Deflated, I took out my phone to call Roshan and let him know that he was waiting for me in a white BMW. It didn't take me long to spot him. I moved forward, meeting him halfway, and extended my hand for a shake. He gladly accepted and led me to the car.

On our way, we talked a lot about random things: the weather, cars, marriage, and much more. He seemed like an easy guy to get along with. A few minutes into the car ride, my phone rang, indicating a call from April.

I pulled my phone out as Roshan said, "Must be April. She's so impatient." I laughed at his comment and picked up the call.

"Yes, Madam?" I asked, trying to contain my excitement.

"Have you reached?" Where are you guys at?" I found myself smiling at her question.

"We are almost there. 15 minutes tops." I said, looking at my watch.

"Okay. I am waiting outside. Come soon." she said, hanging up the phone.

Before I knew it, Roshan was driving down a cobbled path leading to a huge gate.

"Here we are," said Roshan, motioning towards the huge bungalow before us. As he drove forward, the gates opened, and I spotted April standing in the foyer, smiling ear to ear. My smile widened at her sight as I drank in the sight of her fidgety self. Kids were running around the perfectly manicured garden, while elders sat under the trees, enjoying the evening sun. The car came to a stop, and I was quick to get out. April ran towards us as her hair swayed with every step she took. My eyes moved on their own accord, taking in the gorgeous young lady I proudly called my girlfriend. When she came near, her addicting fragrance invaded my senses, making me forget my surroundings for a moment. As she came to stand beside me, I carefully studied her features as if it were the first time I was seeing her. Her long, brown mane was let down freely, falling over her back. Her eyes were lined with black kohl, and her lips were painted with the softest hue of crimson. The dress she wore clung to her frame perfectly, accentuating her features as her innocence embraced a beguiling charm. My emotions were all over the place, and when she hugged me, the closeness and warmth that I have come to love so much engulfed me in a dazzling chimaera. When she tried to pull back, I pulled her more into me, relishing the feeling of my euphoria. She was my destination, my sanity, and my insanity, which I have missed for longer than I realised.

A moment of everything that I missed over the past few days brought me back to my senses, as I became aware of the amused eyes peering at us. I pulled back, took her hand in mine, and raised my eyebrows challengingly at Roshan and Joye, who smiled teasingly at April. She was looking down, her lips set in a wide grin, as more brown locks fell forward, trying to hide her 'tomato face.' She took my backpack from me, trying to hide her embarrassment. Joye was the first one to break the awkward silence.

"Hey, lover boy, didn't you see me?" He asked playfully. I gave him a tight hug and commented.

"I didn't. I missed my queen so much that she stole all my attention." My tone was no better, as I tried to brush off April's embarrassment with playful comments.

"It looks like you're here only for her," teased Joye.

"Why else do you think, huh?" which was partly true too.

"See how the tables turned!" he shot back at me, laughing.

"What's the big deal, anyway?" April huffed in embarrassment; she then twirled as if she would go in alone.

We walked inside, cracking jokes and throwing light insults at each other.

Roshan and Joye were walking ahead of us. I looked around to find no eyes on us and pulled April flush against me, whispering into her ear, "You look beautiful." Her cheeks grew warm and looked more like tomatoes.

She started squirming in my arms, trying to get away. "Leave me. Somebody will see us." She said, looking around to find prying eyes. I left her hand as she pinched my hand and rushed away from me to Roshan and Joye. I laughed heartily and jogged forward to join them.

When we reached the living room, many people were seated. I knew most of them; a few faces were familiar, and a few were unfamiliar.

April's mom stood up as soon as she spotted us. As always, she was draped in a simple sari, pairing the ensemble with minimal jewellery.

"How are you, son?" She asked me, meeting us halfway. Her smile was contagious and showed unadulterated joy.

"I am good," I replied, turning to acknowledge the other people in the room. "Glad to meet you all," I said, nodding my head at no one in particular.

I got a few hellos, heys, and waves in return. April's mom made me sit on one of the seats and served me chamomile tea. People were looking at me like I was some kind of exhibit, and out of discomfort, I gulped the tea down in a jiffy. I looked around, trying to find a way to somehow break the uncomfortable silence.

"Come, let me show you to your room," said April, breaking the silence. She put her coffee mug down and pulled me along, heading towards the staircase. I followed her, feeling grateful for her intervention. We climbed the stairs, and April led me down the corridor. The marble-clad floor was covered with expensive carpets and rugs; the walls were decorated with paintings; and now and then, we passed flower vases holding fresh flowers. She stopped in front of a door at the end of the corridor and opened the door widely for me.

"Here we are," she said, dramatically spreading her hand out. I chuckled lightly and entered the room. April closed the door behind me as I started exploring. The central part of the room was occupied by a huge king-sized bed. A dressing table sat to the left side of the bed, and a 42-inch LED TV hung on the wall. To the left were a corner stand and the bathroom. On the right, next to the dressing table, was a door, lined with dark curtains that led to the balcony. The bed was covered with fresh, white linen, and above the headboard, hung the portrait of two horses. On the right side of the headboard was a shelf packed with books. The walls were painted a light blue, giving the room a warm feeling. On the corner stand sat a vase that held a bunch of carnations. The floor was covered by plush carpet, extending warmth with every step I took. The room was perfect; April made sure of it. I walked around, basking in the evening rays of the sun.

"Nice room," I commented, looking at her reflection in the mirror.

The smile on her face held pride and satisfaction for her work. She walked around, arranging the pillows and opening the blinds and tying them. Seeing her like this, walking around my room and arranging my things, stirred something in me. I was fixed to my spot, unable to act on my thoughts as a sense of urgency coursed through my veins. I walked towards her, as the tension thickened with every step I took. My right hand fell loosely over her waist, pulling her close to me. The sweet smell of lavender invaded my senses as I buried my nose in her hair. As we stood there, overlooking the garden, I lightly traced my hand along her collarbone. She shivered slightly under my touch, gradually easing into its tingling sensation. I dug my hands into my pocket and got out a chain. A small, heart-shaped pendant dangled from the chain. Pushing her hair to her shoulder, I place it around her neck, hooking it from behind. Her right hand came up, lightly tracing the pendant with her fingers, relishing in the feel of the tiny metal piece.

"Take a look in the mirror," I whispered into her hair. She shifted slightly to the side, wanting to see the lavaliere. Her fingers traced its shape, feeling every curve. A contented sigh left her lips as she leaned more into me, our bodies moulding into each other like pieces of a puzzle. Her fingers continued their assault on the metal as our eyes met through the reflection in the mirror. The mood in the room shifted, and carnal cravings laced the air, making the atmosphere dense. I dipped my head into the crook of her neck, never breaking the stare. Her eyes softened, an odd sense of vulnerability and want taking over her features as she felt my hot breath on her shoulder. My hands circled her waist, pulling her more into me, as her eyes closed of their own accord. Her head fell back as I started peppering kisses on her shoulder. Her hands caught hold of my arms in a deathly grip, skimming over my skin in an urgent fashion. My assault made her breath heavy as she struggled to hold in her moans. I nipped and sucked, feeling her go weak in my arms. My stubble rubbed against her neck, making a giggle escape her lips. An overwhelming need took over our hearts as she chanted, "Don't stop." Her palms skimmed over my arms as passion burned high and bright. Her scent teased my senses, aggravating my need. She turned her head sideways, clashing her lips with mine. My grip on her waist loosened as she turned in my arms to face me, granting me full access. Our lips danced in sync of their own, love, longing and need searing into the kiss. Tongues fought for dominance, and grips became more desperate, succumbing to the desire that now led us. I pulled away from the kiss, wanting to see her face. Her naturally pink lips were now red; her cheeks looked more like tomatoes; and her almond eyes were now as wide as saucers.

Her eyes held a strange emotion, a mixture of vulnerability and need. I placed my palm on her cheek, caressing her lips with my thumb.

"You are no less than red wine. Burning, intoxicating, addictive, precious, and beautiful."

Her lips stretched, hinting at a smile of satisfaction.

"And all yours." She repeated after me.

Her eyes closed, giving in to the soft lullaby of my caress, and her lips parted in a passionate abandon. I reclaimed her lips; I was too impatient to hold in the burning fervour. An odd sense of urgency rushed through our veins as we struggled to get rid of the fineries. I unzipped her dress, letting it pool near her feet. Heat coursed from her body to mine, making me hum in pleasure. My fingers skimmed over her unclad body, relishing in the feel of her bare skin and haunting curves. Soft moans left her lips, fuelling my desire to take it to a new high. My fingers slid inside her precious mound, causing her to gasp in pleasure. I traced my fingers across her jewel, as her breath started coming out of her short pants. I whispered sweet nothings into her ear as she writhed in rapture. I slid my fingers inside her, making her roll her head back. Her legs weakened as she held on to my shoulders for support. I continued teasing her with my fingers, enjoying her helpless pants and impetuous moans. I could feel her getting frustrated as she pushed me to the bed and hovered over me. Her fingers fiddled with the buttons on my shirt in an attempt to pry the piece of cloth away. I fell back and watched her tantalising curves, as she fussed over me.

"What? This is not our first time together, yet you are gawking at me as if you've never seen me before." I sat up, pulling her onto my lap, and kissed her throat.

"You always amaze me," I murmured between the kisses. I moved down, as her pink, hardened nipples begged for attention. My lips latched on to it as she wiggled in my lap, unable to resist the torment. I nipped and sucked in an attempt to gratify my unquenchable thirst and keep my hold firm around her waist. I pulled back, feeling content, as her doe eyes gazed into mine, unguarded and pellucid. I hugged her, bringing her form into my warm embrace, as she held on to me like her last straw for life. We stayed like that for some time, unmoving and quiet, relishing in each other's proximity and warmth. I pulled away and placed a kiss on her forehead, only to place my head over her heart. Her heart pounded like it was on fire as the beats played a strange symphony in my ear.

"I missed you so much that it hurt physically. You'll never know how incomplete I felt without you." She muttered as her fingers ran through my hair.

I flipped us over, hovering over her as my eyes searched her face for any kind of apprehension. Finding none, I moved down and parted her legs. Her insides were warm, announcing her readiness to me. I kissed her inner thighs, making her shiver at the sensation. I kissed her flower as she let out a startled gasp. My tongue slid across her clit, tasting her, as she thrashed under my assault. I licked and sucked, pleasuring and teasing her, loving the way she went putty in my arms. She tried to move away in an attempt to escape the torment, only to be stopped by my grip on her hips. Her hands caught hold of the bed sheet as she tried to thrash her legs around. Innocent almond eyes were now clouded with lust as she cried out, pleasure hitting her in waves.

"Please," she pleaded, begging me to give her the release she wished for. I kissed her, unable to wait any longer, pouring my emotions into the kiss. I pushed my shaft against her entrance, as our sounds of pleasure were muffled by the kiss we shared. Together, we climbed the ecstatic peak, shattering into pure bliss.

I plopped on the bed by her side as she turned to me with a goofy smile.

"Tired?" she asked, earning a hearty chuckle from me.

I turned to the side, propping my head on my palm. "What do you think?" I asked, winking at her.

I laid down, pulling April close to me. Her head lay on my chest, and her hands made doodles on my chest. I wrapped my hands around her waist, enjoying the cuddle. We lay there, not speaking much.

"What is bothering you? Are you tired?" April asked, breaking the silence.

I looked down to see her eyebrows furrowed with worry. "Baby, trust me. I am not tired. Just thinking about Ben." I kissed her forehead, smoothing the lines on her forehead. "How can God be so cruel as to inflict such pain on him?" I asked, letting out a sigh.

"What happened?" April prodded, wanting to know more.

I spooned her from behind, saying nothing, as silence enveloped us like a cold blanket.

The odour of her skin tranquil my soul,

As the delightful night spent with her.

The radiance of her eyes captive me,

Fiddle me and whisper in my ears,

You are the one I crave for.

| PART 3

Life is a journey. Here, you meet people, both good and bad. Some stay, while others pass by. Some leave without saying goodbye, and some barge in without greetings. Some evoke pleasant feelings; some inflict pain. It's so easy to be misguided, and often, we end up chasing the wrong - person. It is a mutual choice between two individuals, a duel of want and need, companionship and discord. But what's life without pain? We would never know what happiness is without the shadow of pain.

What binds two individuals together? What makes them endure all their misery for one another? Perhaps it is pure instinct, an animalistic attraction, or even a fleeting emotion. Maybe it's a feeling that is so unpredictable and limitless that it is not countable or measurable and knows no bounds. A feeling they weren't aware of yet, that unconsciously made them behave like fools just to please each other, and that was so obvious to the people all around them. Deep down, they knew it; they knew that there wouldn't be anybody else ever again and that their fates were woven together now. And they wouldn't hesitate to die for each other.

Is it love? This feeling that makes you throb, pure and raw like an open wound?

Ben's thoughts were scattered as he strutted down the hallway. An odd feeling of tranquillity bewitched him, waking unknown thoughts. People passed by as the clatter of their shoes went unnoticed. The campus was truly picturesque, as one would see in the movies. Trees lined the boundaries, and the vibe was refreshing and enriching. A breeze blew past, cooling his heart and body alike.

"Hey, stop," a familiar voice commanded from behind.

The comfort he felt was much more tempting than the annoying voice. So, he walked faster, pretending not to hear that.

"Ahh. It's hurting. Please stop." The same voice sounded again. He was annoyed. Why would I stop? He thought, hoping to vent his anger on the person, and he turned around, ready to pounce on the annoying owner of the voice.

"Apoorva?" he asked, feeling baffled. Any trace of annoyance left him, his heart soaring at the mere sight of her.

"Yeah. Apoorva. My hair is stuck in the zip of your backpack," she said, as she tried to untangle her hair.

"Oh!! I'm sorry. I didn't notice," he said, as he untangled her hair from the zipper.

Apoorva looked radiant, like always. Her long hair was let down in waves. Her face was free from any substance, nothing but the flushed red blush on the pale canvas from all the hassle of the morning commute, and the dark brown dress she wore accentuated her curves, the dark hue a stark contrast against her pale pallor. A black spot marked the clear skin of her chin, drawing his attention to it.

Is that a mole or a dot of kajal to shoo away evil eyes? He wondered, finding the spot oddly addicting. A shake from Apoorva pulled him out of his trance, making him wonder if he said that out loud. Yet her eyes remained passive, an innocent smile plastered on her lips.

"Anybody home?" Apoorva asked, waving her hands on his face.

"Nothing," he replied with a smile.

Appu," he heard a girl shout. "Come on. We'll be late for class." Another voice shouted, making her head turn.

"See ya later," Apoorva yelled, jogging towards her friends.

What are you? Why do I feel so strange around you? You stir my soul with just your presence. What is this feeling? Is this love? If yes, I am utterly, deeply, and wholly in love with you, Apoorva. He chanted in his head, watching her walk away.

Words seemed to fail him as he thought about their short yet sweet encounters. Apoorva moved him like no other, baring him open for her, even if she didn't know that. Love seemed to do that to him, as he danced to the tunes of his heart, ignoring his mind altogether.

A harsh pat on his shoulder brought him out of his reverie.

"Hey man!!! Jeff here. And you?" he asked, surprising Ben. The guy was brutally straightforward. No small talk or getting-to-know-each-other crap.

"Benedict, Ben for short," he said, extending his hand for a handshake.

"Brothers, bro. Brothers. No handshakes," he said, bumping shoulders with Ben's.

Ben nodded, loving Jeff's character. He was so lively and loud. So full of life. That itself lured Ben in, wanting to befriend the guy. Jeff was doing more than half the job. He didn't have to worry.

"Look around, Bro. Colourful, isn't it?" Jeff asked, making him raise his eyebrow in question.

"Bro, more colours mean more girls. You still have a long way to go." He said, making Ben throw his head back in a burst of hearty laughter.

"I saw you talking to that girl," Jeff said, making Ben tense. He was not ready to share his feelings with anyone yet. His feelings needed a lot of thought and contemplation. And he intended to do just that.

"Which girl?" Ben asked, feigning innocence.

"That girl. Beautiful girl. The one with long, wavy hair? Dark brown dress? Doe-shaped eyes? Hot as hell, girl? Ring a bell?" He asked, his expression turning comical with every passing moment.

"Yeah. Yeah. That girl." Ben said, unable to resist any longer.

"Girlfriend?" Jeff asked.

"What? No." Ben exclaimed, his voice rising by an octave.

"Soon to be, then. How do you know her if she is not, you know, your girlfriend?" Jeff asked, quoting the word girlfriend on the air.

"Neighbours. She lives a few blocks away from my place." Ben replied awkwardly.

"So, you mean, you talk to all the girls in your neighbourhood like that?" Jeff asked, wiggling his eyebrows at Ben.

"Go away, you scoundrel," Ben said as Jeff started running to escape Ben's assault.

45

"Go away, you scoundrel," Ben said as Jeff started running to escape Ben's assault.

College was Ben's heaven. His efforts and commitment made him their star athlete and the most valued player on the football team. Ben was very confident about the sport, and every time the team was in trouble, they'd turn to him, seeking his help.

"You get to take the penalty shot. You are aware of how important the game is. You are our finest, and we need your best." Jeff shouted from across the field, once again putting the responsibility on him. He loved it and revelled in the attention it got him. Playing for his team, the cheers, the shout outs, and the prayers boosted him to no end. Over the past few weeks, Jeff has become a good friend of his, a brother from another mother. He supported Ben like no other, was his personal vault to keep secrets.

When the game was over, Jeff decided that he wanted to quench the feeling of fire swirling in his stomach. Though he did nothing more than sit on the side-lines watching them play and was hooting at every move they made, he was hungry enough to swallow an elephant. So, he dragged Ben to their college cafeteria so that he could have his fill at Ben's expense. It was like Ben was bribing him to keep his secrets. Ben would buy him food—more than enough food—his favourite food and then start talking about Apoorva. Jeff would sit there and listen to him, mostly stuffing his face with samosas and pakoras. Occasionally, he'd drop in snarky comments, which would make Ben's mood sour. If his comments are too sour to handle, Ben would even eat up the entire order while Jeff would watch on. So, Jeff always tries to keep a lid on his comments. The keyword being 'try'.

They went inside the cafeteria and sat in their usual seats. The one by the window, at the end of the cafeteria. When not on the field, Ben liked to keep his awesomeness to himself, wanting to stay out of silly dramas. That's why he always preferred this seat. Nobody would notice him that easily in the cafeteria in one glance if he sat there. At the same time, he could see everything that happened in the cafeteria without anyone knowing. Just as Jeff came to the table with a huge tray full of food and drinks, Ben noticed a group of girls enter the cafeteria. What pulled his gaze to the group was Apoorva's loud laughter, which rang around the cafeteria like music to his ears. They came in and sat at a table near the counter.

"Four Tropicanas and one brownie, please." She yelled at the guy on the counter and looked back at her friends. She saw a guy pass by their table and bump into Niha. The guy started walking ahead without an apology for his actions.

"Are you blind? Didn't you see her?" shouted Apoorva.

Ben watched the drama unfold from another table. Verbal tiffs like these were common in the college cafeteria. Normally, a large gathering would follow, with people taking sides and throwing insults at each other. Fistfights were rare. So, when he saw the guy raising his hand at her, he saw red. In a flash, Ben stood beside Apoorva, blocking the other guy's punch and landing one on his face. The guy fell back, holding onto his face in pain. When Ben turned to Apoorva, her eyes were shut tightly and her hands covered her ears.

"Are you okay?" He asked as she opened her eyes slowly, looking around to assess the scene.

"Yeah. The guy is an ass!!!" she said, making him smile.

"Who the hell are you? Trying to be a hero? Newsflash, brother. We didn't need your help to resolve this."

Ben turned around to see Febin standing up, still nursing his wounded ego.

"You." Ben started shouting.

"Benedict and Febin!" the principal's voice echoed sternly. "What on earth are you two doing, fighting like this in the middle of the day? This is completely unacceptable behaviour. If I ever catch you fighting again, both of you will face serious consequences, including suspension. And Ben, being a star athlete and winning championships doesn't give you a free pass to cause trouble. I won't tolerate it. Now, enough of this nonsense. Both of you, go to your classes immediately."

Feeling scolded, Ben and Febin reluctantly left the premises, shooting each other one last glare. As Febin walked out of the cafeteria towards his friends, Ben exited the area to find Apoorva waiting for him. The scolding from the principal had left an uneasy tension in the air, and Ben knew he needed to handle such situations more carefully in the future.

She stood up as he approached her. Her head hung low as she murmured, "Sorry. Because of me..."

Ben held his hand up, making her stop. "It's okay. I did what I felt was right. Leave it." She finally lifted her head, a hesitant smile playing on her lips.

From there, they parted ways as Apoorva rushed to catch up with her friends for lunch.

Their lunchtime was Apoorva's time to catch up with her friends. They laughed and celebrated their happiness, washed away their sorrows and found support in each other's presence.

"Listen, girls. I've got something to ask." Apoorva said, shifting her friends' attention from food to her.

"What yaar? Let's finish that chicken tikka and then, ask anything." Niha said, trying to go back to devouring her delicacy.

"No tikka for you until you hear me out," Apoorva said, taking it away from her.

"Hypocrite," murmured Niha.

"So, I was thinking...." started Apoorva.

"Don't just think. Spit it out. My tikka is calling out for me." Niha said, making Apoorva scoff.

"What if Ben comes near me and confesses his undying love for me?" Apoorva asked, sighing dreamily.

"Ha!!! What a dream!!!! Did you take my tikka away for voicing out this stupid dream? NOT. GONNA. HAPPEN." Niha shouted, snatching the box from her hand.

"You and your tikka." Go away." Apoorva said, thrusting the box back to Niha.

"Nice dream, Appu. In fact, every girl on this campus dreams of this. But it will not work for you." Sminu said, making Apoorva's face fall.

"But why? What's wrong with me?" She asked, suddenly feeling self-conscious.

"You do not talk to him. A few greetings here and there don't count. Talk to him. How's he supposed to make a move if you don't talk to him?" Sminu asked.

"I am scared. What if he just likes me as a friend?" Apoorva asked, her voice low with tension.

"What? Are you blind or something? Have you seen the guy's face when he sees you? It lights up like its Diwali night." Niha shouted, stuffing more chicken into her mouth.

"She may be a greedy cow when it comes to tikka, but what she said just now is true. I also think that Ben likes you. It's very evident from his looks." Sminu said, making Niha nod her head.

I should make a move. Apoorva thought. *I should make a move quickly so that everybody knows he's mine. But how? So, all those dumb heads would back off of my man's tail. And if they still don't get the point, I'll personally mess those bitches up...*

"Apoorva, why are you stabbing the table with my pen?" Niha broke her off from the train of thoughts as Apoorva glared down at the table and the pen, which now sported a bent nib from the aggressive stabbing.

Sminu had confusion and a bit of worry written all over her face.

"It owed me money," Apoorva explained with a frown and stabbed the table one last time before giving the pen away to Niha.

"Didn't you hear the bell? Lunchtime is over, girls," their teacher said, making them look up.

"Miss Poker Face is here, girls," Emma murmured under her breath, as the girls tried hard to keep their laughter in.

"Anyway, I was here to inform you that we'll be practising the drama for the college day celebration. Are you interested?" The teacher asked, making Apoorva roll her eyes. Her friends have always been fascinated by the performing arts. She, on the other hand, didn't even have a single artistic bone in her body.

"Not interested," Apoorva shouted. She picked up her bag and walked out, knowing that none of her friends would follow.

She walked, enjoying the warmth of the extended branches of the peepal trees. The edges of their campus were lined by different trees, extending unconventional warmth and never-ending glee.

Ben was standing at his usual spot when he saw Apoorva trotting along with the shadows. Getting her alone, away from her friends, was a dream come true. Apoorva always had her friends trailing her; the four Musketeers were rarely spotted alone. Ben jogged towards her, hoping to talk to her and get to know her better.

"Hey, Apoorva!" he said, grabbing her attention from the reverie she was in.

"Hello," she said, sitting down on the wooden desk.

"Why are you here, alone?" He asked.

"Not interested in drama. I have never been a big fan of the performing arts. Sucks for me, because all my friends are, so, here I am, lamenting over the absence of my non-existent inner performer." she said, making him laugh. Never in his life had he heard something so sarcastic. Everything about her seemed to make him feel light, funny, and happy.

"What about a quiz? A little birdie told me that you are an ace when it comes to quiz competitions." Ben said, praying for her to say yes.

"There's a quiz competition?" "Why was I not informed?" she asked, perplexed.

"Maybe you missed the announcement. Before you start looking for a partner, let me tell you that I am free. I have been hunting for one, and the fact that my partner is going to be a very beautiful girl doesn't hurt." He winked at her.

"Ha!!! Don't flatter me." Apoorva said, making him pout.

"Okay. I'm game. "Now, whom should I report to?" she asked.

"Find Rijo sir, and tell him that you are pairing up with me," he said, excitement bubbling up in his head.

"Sure. Then I shall go and find him. We don't want somebody else to steal my handsome partner now, don't we?" Apoorva said, making him laugh harder.

Days passed by. Every day brought new challenges and took him one step closer to his dream, Apoorva. They were good friends now, thanks to the quiz competition. Sometimes, they'd even have coffee together at the nearby Starbucks. The semi-final round of the football tournament was here. Ben was confident. He and his team had worked hard; something has got to come out of it. Students filled the galleries, bringing the stadium to life. High-energy music blared from the speakers as the commotion increased with every passing second.

The first half of the game, though exciting, did not shake the net for either team. During the break time before the commencement of the second half, Jeff entered the room, clapping his hands and demanding the team's attention.

"Today is the day, guys. You've been working so long for this. We can't afford to let it go down the drain. So, once you are out there, play with everything you've got because we need to win this match. Cheer up, because we only have the second half left. Your standing among other teams will be determined by this," he said, as players started fist-bumping each other and jogged out of the room.

The second half of the game often brought the onlookers to the edge. But, once again, no goals were scored.

Finally, in the last few minutes of injury time, their team decided to hand over the responsibility to their best player—Ben. The free kick they got was their only chance to prove their worth. Anything short of victory was unacceptable. In situations like these, he was the one everyone would turn to. Ben was a player who knew how to play right, no matter what challenges the circumstances posed. His fellow teammates surrounded him, motivating him to no end and boosting his confidence to a whole new level. Finally, when his time came, he jogged to his spot, accompanied by hoots and hollers. As soon as he was at his spot, positioning himself for the free-kick, the gallery fell silent. Besides the occasional hoots, no sound was to be heard. Ben looked around, feeling the eyes of the people who badly wanted him to succeed. He was carrying the burden of the hopes of an entire college. He knew that. He couldn't fail, for that would be the failure of all those who believed in him. Closing his eyes, he sent a quick prayer upwards. After a second, when he opened his eyes, Ben knew that he would not fail. With newfound confidence, he ran forward and kicked the ball high. Everything was on hold for a moment. The world around him stilled, all eyes following the ball's movement. The defending players jumped high with the ball, high enough for one of them to block. He closed his eyes, unable to watch the scene unfold. After a moment, the gallery was roaring, with energy like no other reverberating through the field. Ben opened his eyes slowly to see his teammates running up to him crazily. The defending team members sat on the ground; dejection clear in their stance. One of his team members tackled him to the ground with happiness, and the rest of them piled on top of him.

The match had always been theirs. Ben knew that. He hadn't spent so much time for nothing. His well-placed free kick was their tiebreaker, their one-way ticket to the finals. People started crowding him, congratulating him for his work, and appreciating his effort. His eyes sought only one person as he looked around, trying to spot her, blindly mumbling thank you to every compliment that came his way. "She promised to come to the match. She wouldn't break it, would she?" he asked himself.

When the hollers and shouts came to an end, he walked out of the stadium, feeling dejected. As he passed by the gallery, he spotted a figure at the entrance, leaning on the door. His steps picked up speed, excitement spreading through his soul once again. He jogged towards her as she turned towards him, a smile lighting up her soft features.

"Why weren't you here for the match? I expected you to come." Ben said, his voice thick with emotion.

She tucked a strand of hair behind her ear, a shy smile stretching across her face.

"Who said I didn't watch? I even came to the dressing room to congratulate you. But so many people were surrounding you, and I thought to greet you later." She said, looking at him warily. He was panting hard, and sweat streamed down his face incessantly.

"That was not an issue. You should've come inside," he said, making her smile wider.

"It's okay. Now I get to congratulate you alone. You will only hear my cheers." she said, making him laugh.

"This is for your awesome performance on the field," she said, handing him an energy drink.

Ben smiled to himself.

"Got it for me. But then I just couldn't greet the star athlete empty-handed," she added, as he opened the bottle and chugged down the liquid.

Apoorva was feeling chattier than he could handle.

"Well, this may inflate your ego even more. But I missed you yesterday. You were busy practising, and I didn't have the heart to take that away from you." She said as he threw his bottle into the dustbin with the precision of a basket player. He smiled with pride as the bottle landed perfectly in the bin.

"Why? Is my charm that irresistible? I always knew I had it in me, but knowing that you fell for it is a different feeling. It feeds my already 'bigger than earth' ego." Ben joked, feeling lighter than ever.

Both of them walked out of the stadium, enjoying each other's proximity.

"The sky is so beautiful today." Apoorva commended the clear blue sky.

"Do you know the story of the sky, the rain, and the earth?" Ben asked, making her curious.

"No. What is that?" Her voice was heavy with curiosity.

"The sky is showing his love for the earth through the rain. Earth responds by blooming more flowers." Ben replied, his voice so serious that Apoorva believed him.

"Really?" she quipped.

"What are you, a dummy? How could you believe that?" Ben asked incredulously.

Apoorva's eyes widened alarmingly, and she punched him on the shoulder, laughing at her stupidity.

That evening ended with them parting ways half-heartedly after a lengthy stroll.

The morning came, opening doors to new experiences to look forward to. Ben was uncharacteristically happy. He was bursting with energy to share the reason for his happiness with Jeff. He deserved to know. He was his soul brother, after all.

"Guess what she asked me yesterday?" Ben dreamily sighed, falling back on the lawn.

"Your brain? Tell her that you lost it years ago." Jeff said, making him annoyed.

"Go die, you idiot." He said, kicking his friend.

"Sorry, sorry, sorry..." Jeff chanted, making Ben stop.

"So, *what did she ask*?"

"She asked me to go out with her on Friday. Isn't that awesome? Something worth celebrating?" Ben asked as Jeff looked at him as if he had grown two heads.

"As a friend, right? Why are you so thrilled about it?" Jeff asked as Ben's smile widened.

"Because today we may be friends. Later, romance will find its way into our relationship, making us lovers. Then, in the future, we may share life. Let me tell you the truth. My poor heart is in love, dear friend." Ben chanted away dreamily, as if in a trance.

"With whom, dude?" Jeff asked comically.

"With your grandma," Ben screamed angrily, turning heads their way from different corners of the lawn. Jeff smiled awkwardly, embarrassed by his actions.

"But why Ben? Tell her how you feel. What's the point in hiding your feelings?" Jeff asked, rocking back and forth like a pendulum.

"Jeff, I love her. I really love her. Anything she can give me is my elixir. Even if it's just friendship. But losing her altogether because I couldn't wait any longer would get me nowhere, leaving me to rot in my personal hell. I can't take that." Ben confessed; his eyes fixed on the clear blue sky.

"Oh, Romeo. She won't reject you. Girls will die to get a glance from you. You are that popular. Why would she reject someone like that? And not just that. Apoorva is a unique girl. If you could win her over, I'd say that you hit the jackpot. Trust me, her rejection is going to be the least of your problems." Jeff chatted away, stating a million reasons for everything to go right.

"Really? Do you think so?" He asked, suspicion lacing his voice.

"You fool. Just go and share your feelings with her." Jeff cheered, making Ben laugh.

"Well, tell me why my heart chose her out of all those girls—as you say—fawning over my hot ass," Ben asked, his cocky self-coming into play.

"How would I know?" Jeff asked. Something wetted his shirt as he talked. His hand grazed the side of his shirt to feel something gooey and sticky.

"Shit man!!! It's shit!!!" Jeff yelled, a disgusted look crossing his face.

"The crow sure knows its latrine." Ben sang, laughing at his friend's misfortune. "The heart really doesn't know when to stop. I see her everywhere. My mind keeps whispering her name. Ah…. love sure is maddening." He mumbled dreamily, a sigh of contentment leaving his lips.

"What are you? Bipolar? You're insulting me and professing your love for her in the same sentence. Hell, man!!!!! What kind of friend are you?" Jeff complained, his voice rising by an octave.

"Ah…love is like that. You can't help but spend your time thinking about that one person. Friends don't have that power over each other." Ben sang, mischief brimming in his voice.

The pendulum of life oscillates between jubilant and dispiriting moments as we blindly search for happiness, refusing to acknowledge the balance that sorrows bring.

Ben loved sports. Sports gave him the title of a star, and he was practically worshipped every time he was spotted on campus. The adrenaline rushes those cheers gave, the feeling of liberation, those hoots and hollers—he loved it all. Sports day, indeed, was his day. Ben reached the campus that day feeling all pumped up and ready for some action.

He stepped into the track as the scorching sun shone high in the sky. Beads of sweat ran through his body, making him smile. Pop songs blared through the speakers as the crowd roared and went haywire with excitement.

"Ben... Ben..." Jeff's voice was barely audible through the hubbub. Ben waved his hand in the air, shouting, "Over here." Jeff jogged to him, an odd sense of urgency in his steps.

"What's got your ugly ass on fire?" Ben asked, resuming his stretches.

"Your handsome ass too will catch fire in a minute." Jeff shot back, giving his friend a stink eye.

Ben stood straight, watching his friend with apprehension. "And why is that?" he asked, suspicion lacing his voice.

"ApoorvaisbettingwithFebinonyoureventandifyouloseshewould'veto kisshim." Jeff rasped out a breath.

Ben looked comically at his friend to see him heaving. "What was that? Repeat that. This time, with proper punctuation," he demanded, as Jeff scrunched his eyebrows.

"No man!!!! Don't make me do this. I can handle your jolly ass, not you're seething ass," he pleaded, searching Ben's eyes for a twinge of sympathy. Ben raised an eyebrow at his friend, making Jeff sigh in defeat.

"Apoorva is betting with Febin on your event. If you lose, she'd have to kiss him." Jeff said, eyeing Ben warily.

"Hell!!!!! What was she thinking? Despite the truth that I'm going to win no matter what, she just can't go around betting like that." Ben turned around to see his friend looking weirdly at him.

"Whoa. You and your narcissistic ass." Jeff joked, patting Ben's shoulder.

"I'm not being narcissistic. I'm being confident. There's a difference," he said, his eyes wandering around the field.

"Here comes your Anarkali. I'm officially off the hook now that she's here. You can sort it among yourselves." Jeff said, pointing to a very nervous Apoorva, who was timidly approaching them. He waved at her and jogged back to the gallery.

"Hi Ben," she mumbled, casting her eyes down.

"What?" Ben spat, his emotions getting the best of him.

"I am betting with Febin and..." She mumbled, unable to speak further.

"Why is it so difficult for you to speak up now? It wasn't that difficult when you ran your mouth idiotically at Febin," Ben asked, anger clouding his voice.

"I.... I am sorry. Please don't be mad." she pleaded, his eyes softening at the sight.

"I am not mad at you. I'm just annoyed, that you put a bet on something as uncertain as this. What were you thinking? I could be out of form or just out of luck. What would you have done then?" he asked, his mind playing a million scenarios of him losing.

"But you are neither. You are at your best. Please, Ben, I trust you. You have to win this race for me." Her hands grabbed him as she directed her best puppy eyes at him.

Ben smiled unknowingly. The girl had him wrapped around her pinkie finger, whether she knew it or not.

"Yeah… Yeah... I'll try my level best. No promises, though. Besides, what's in it for me if I win this race?" He asked, his eyebrows raising a little.

"Your best is all I ask for. And if you win this race, you can ask me for anything," Apoorva said, her smile bigger than his.

"Anything?" Ben asked.

"Anything." She asserted.

"I'm counting on you on that one," Ben said, pushing her towards the gallery. She walked away, a shy smile gracing her lips.

Just then, the speaker blared, "Final call for participants of the 400-metre running race." Ben spared one last look at Apoorva's retreating back and took his position.

Competitors, on your mark." Ben looked forward to seeing Apoorva and Jeff cheering for him.

She looked so innocent, and childlike, cheering for him like nothing else mattered. At that moment, he knew that he just couldn't let her down. If he was out of luck, he'd have to make his luck and win. He just couldn't let a moron like Febin kiss Apoorva. That ass didn't even deserve to stand in her way. A whistle blared, making Ben set his eyes forward, on the finish line. "Get.........." the speaker blared. A bead of sweat rolled down his forehead. "...Set" The words seemed to take forever to come out. The sweat bead streamed down his nose, reaching the tip, begging to fall. A gunshot was heard, making Ben sprint forward. The sweat bead fell as Ben took off with all his might.

He ran, his mind, muddled with thoughts of Febin kissing Apoorva. Halfway through the race, he heard the speakers shout, "Looks like Febin is going to win this year's athletic championship. His pace is no less than a professional's. Way to go, Febin!" Ben didn't hear what else was being announced through the speaker. He couldn't let Febin win. With that thought, he quickened his pace, easily outrunning two people ahead of him. Now, he only had Febin to take over. Adrenaline rushed through his body, making him run past his opponent, once again proving to be the star athlete they always named him to be. He ran like lightning and reached the finish line, finishing in a moment of glory a few seconds before Febin.

He cast a spell of prayer upwards and turned around to meet a hollering Jeff and an ecstatic Apoorva.

"If this isn't the one and only Ben!!!!" Jeff shouted, hugging him tighter. "Ewwww.... Man!!!! You are drenched. Now I gotta change too." Jeff shouted; his disgust clear on his face.

"Oye, who asked you to hug me? I must take a bath now that you hugged me." Ben shouted back, embarrassed at his friend's insult.

He then turned to Apoorva, who was laughing her ass off watching their banter. "Happy?" Ben asked mischief marring his smile.

"Insanely so!" Apoorva answered, her smile mirroring his, a twinge of shyness enveloping it. In a moment, her arms wrapped around him, his hands following on their own accord. A blanket of bliss fell over them as they stood there, uncaring and unaware of the stares that came their way. Jeff's jaw dropped open; their PDA was too much for him to handle.

He whispered into Ben's ear, "You are in public. Tone it down a bit, will ya? The entire college is watching you."

Apoorva pulled back abruptly, shocking Ben. Her shy eyes scanned the crowd and landed on Ben's.

"I.....I'm sorry. I didn't mean to... I just... out of excitement..." Apoorva struggled to find the right words.

"Hey... hey... hey... breathe... You did nothing wrong.... It was just a hug. There's nothing to worry about." Ben said, trying to calm her down.

"Yeah. Thanks for your understanding. See you later." Apoorva said, leaving the ground in a hurry.

Love is addictive. The search for it never ends. The thirst for it is never quenched. Pain is just the way to feel love, a reminder to not let go of what we already have.

The next few days went by like a breeze. Ben was happy that he could help Apoorva stand her ground and fight back when it came to Febin. It made him happy like nothing else. Apoorva was becoming bolder, and he was ecstatic about it. He wanted her to not crunch under bullying. With the victory that they gained over Febin a few days ago, everything seemed much brighter for him. He was happy with everything that was unfolding around him. Every moment was joyful, and he couldn't appreciate life any more.

Ben was in the cafeteria sipping a strong, black coffee. As he raised the cup to his lips, he saw Apoorva entering the cafeteria. His eyes watched her movements like a hawk, uncaring of the creepy vibe it gave off.

"Man..." Jeff whispered near his ear. Ben didn't respond. He watched her move across the cafeteria to the order counter. "Man... You are giving off creepy vibes. Stop following her with your eyes. You look no less than a serial killer." Jeff screamed into his ear. Ben's trance broke, and he turned towards his friend, who was smiling like a fool.

"You know what? Just forget it. You won't understand. But one thing: If I am a serial killer, then you are my accomplice in crimes. My doom is yours too. And, stop screaming into my ear." Ben said, his face contorting with irritation.

"What? I just saved you from being a creepy stalker. If you want to talk to her.... let me show you what to do." Jeff said, not completing his sentence. He waved his hand high to catch Apoorva's attention. When she didn't notice, he yelled for her, making her look around.

"Here," Jeff said from across the café, waving his hand. Her eyes found Ben's, a smile stretching on her lips. She walked towards them, smiling widely.

"Bro... Now the ball is in your court. Make your move." Jeff whispered in Ben's ears. Ben nodded, trying to calm his frantic heart.

Apoorva stood near their table, feeling awkward. Jeff nudged Ben's arm lightly, prompting him to say something. Ben opened and closed his mouth, saying nothing, like a fish out of water. Silence fell over them, irritating Jeff to no end.

"Sit down, Apoorva. We have extra chairs." Jeff said, motioning to the chair, effectively breaking whatever trance the lovesick couple was in. Apoorva nodded her head at him and pulled out a chair for her to sit in.

"So? What would you like to drink? Tea or coffee?" Ben asked, initiating small talk between them.

"Two burgers, a sandwich, one plate of nuggets, and a passion fruit mojito for me," Jeff yelled, making Ben turn towards his friend.

"What?" Ben asked, raising his eyebrows. "Are you planning to eat the entire cafeteria?"

"Dude. Don't worry about the money. Today, I am not going to gorge on your account. We are going to gorge, and it's all on her." he said, pointing to Apoorva. "Isn't it Apoorva?" he asked, smiling widely at her.

Her eyes widened at his comment as she looked around, searching for an exit. Ben chuckled at her expression, causing her to smile half-heartedly.

"Today, it's on me, Jeff," he announced, not taking his eyes off her. "Our Apoorva here is not interested in buying us food. Isn't it Apoorva?" he asked, making her squirm.

"No," she said almost immediately. "I just.... I'll treat you guys some other day," she mumbled, looking away.

"No worries. I just need food. Who pays for it is none of my concern." Jeff said, rocking in his chair. Ben snickered and went to order for them.

"When is the final tournament?" Apoorva asked, as soon as Ben returned to the table with their orders. Jeff started stuffing his face with food, not waiting for the both of them.

"Dates are not yet announced. But, most probably, they'll conduct it during the next week." He said, before asking, Apoorva, "if I ask you something personal, will you tell me?" Her eyes sought his, hope dancing in both their eyes. She nodded her head, yes, making him suck his breath in.

"Do you..." he shook his head in an attempt to muster more courage. "Do you like anyone? As in, like, 'love'?" His choice of words was foreign to his own ears.

Jeff laughed out loudly, as some burger pieces flew out of his mouth and fell on Ben's lap.

"What?" Ben asked, suddenly annoyed by his friend's tantrums.

"Nothing. Sorry. It just happened." He apologised and once again stuffed his face with food before saying, "You continue with your 'like of love' talk."

Ben turned his attention to Apoorva, who was blushing furiously. "I am sorry if I asked something wrong," Ben said, trying to coax an answer out of her.

"No, no, Ben." You didn't ask anything wrong. "Actually, I like someone from our college," she said, her eyes twinkling at the mere mention of the guy.

Ben's hands formed into a fist under the table. His lips stretched into a forced smile. "Oh. I didn't know. Well, how is he? Smart? Handsome?" he asked, muttering curses under his breath.

"He's a sweet guy. Looks tough on the outside, but is soft on the inside. So smart and handsome. All in all, he's so cool." She said it dreamily.

"Late bro. You are very, very late. But who is this fool who captured her heart before you?" Jeff murmured into Ben's ear.

"Shut up, you pig. If not, I'll kill you with my bare hands." Ben warned his friend, who pushed his chair further away from Ben's.

Apoorva talked nonstop about the guy she liked. Ben's patience was thinning with every passing second. He badly wanted to know the guy's name, but he was not sure what he'd do to him once he identified the man who had Apoorva's heart in his hands.

As Apoorva continued praising her love interest, a girl from her class rushed towards their table.

"Hey Apoorva," she said, greeting her hastily.

Hey, Daksha, why are you here? Where's your gang?" Apoorva asked, looking around.

"Didn't you hear the bell ring? Our professor has been screaming for your project from the very moment he stepped into our class. Go and submit It." the girl said, rushing out of the cafeteria as soon as she relayed the message.

Apoorva started collecting her things from the table in a hurry. "Me and my pea-sized brain. Don't know what I was thinking lounging back and not caring about the rest of the world," she mumbled to herself, trying to fit her things in the bag. Once done, she turned to the duo, who were watching her with amused eyes, and said, "So sorry, guys. We have to cut this meeting short. Treat me to tea some other time, when a dragon is not breathing down my neck. Bye." With that, she turned around and scurried out without sparing another glance.

Jeff's phone was vibrating on the table, while he was stuffing his face with the burger. Seeing him in no mood to pick up the call, Ben peered into the display to see Jeff's mom's face flashing on it. Though hesitantly, he nudged Jeff to get his attention.

"What?" Jeff was irritated. By then, the call had been cut. The phone started vibrating frequently, indicating the swarm of messages that were being received.

"It is your mom, Jeff!" Ben said, cautiously.

"You know why I don't pick up her calls, don't you?" Jeff asked, turning his head to his friend. Ben nodded solemnly.

"Then why are you disturbing me over her calls, Ben?" Jeff asked, pain lacing his voice. "You are so lucky, Ben. Your parents love each other. They love you. But, look at mine. Although divorced, they still quarrel whenever they get a chance. They blame each other for ruining their lives. And, in the end, they call me. Not to ask my whereabouts, but to complain about the other." Ben placed a hand on Jeff's shoulder, who was on the verge of shedding tears.

"They must have met each other in today's meeting. Their ego wouldn't let them leave without sharing a few curse words. You know what? Today, I am staying at my dad's. Last night, Mom was rambling about how she'd outsmart Dad today. Today, I'll hear him ramble about Mom's inadequate behaviour. I enjoy myself only when I am here. So, please, don't ask me to take their calls. Let me stay happy while I am here." Jeff said pleadingly. He took his drink in one hand and walked out, leaving the vibrating phone for Ben to take.

Ben desperately wanted to knock some sense into Jeff's parents. Their being divorced was fine. Jeff was in agreement with the fact. But quarrelling at every chance they got and dragging Jeff into it was unacceptable. He didn't think the impact their quarrels had on Jeff's life was known to them. Ben took the vibrating phone and switched it off, stopping its incessant quiver. He put it in his back pocket and ran up to Jeff in an attempt to bring himself back.

An hour later, Ben was sitting under the massive peepal tree that stood at the centre of their campus. The campus looked deserted with almost all the students in classes. Ben fell back, lying down on the lawn. His thoughts were going haywire. The thought of Apoorva loving someone else pained him to no end. What if the guy was someone close to him? He knew that he'd do something rash. His inner voice was pestering him to find the guy and beat him black and blue so that Apoorva would stop loving him because of his ugly face. But he knew that it would hurt Apoorva. She may even stop talking to him. He couldn't bear to not talk to her. No matter who she loved—even if it was not him—he loved her. If not as her boyfriend, he wanted to continue to talk to her as just a friend. His thoughts were scattered as he closed his eyes to calm his raging heart. If Apoorva loved someone else, he hoped with all his heart for the guy to reciprocate her feelings. Even if she was not his, he wanted her to be the happiest woman on the face of the earth.

Apoorva found him under the peepal tree, lying on the lawn with his hands folded behind his head and his eyes closed. She walked towards him and towered over him, blocking the angry rays of the sun and admiring every contour of his face. Ben was a handsome man, and she loved him like no other. Loving someone before getting to know them was strange. Apoorva knew that. Yet she couldn't help but fall for him. It was not his star persona or dashing looks that drew her to him. Under all those layers, she found a man who was kind and humble with a heart of gold. She was so immersed in her thoughts that she didn't see Ben opening his eyes.

Ben looked at the girl who towered over him, deep in her thoughts. She looked like an angel. That was when the realisation hit him hard. *She did not belong to him. She likes someone else.* The thought angered him to no end. His face contorted with annoyance at her. Without bothering to sit straight, he asked, "What are you looking so keenly at? Immersed in the thoughts of your boyfriend?" A hint of sarcasm panned his voice.

The question was enough to break her out of the reverie she was in. She shook her head, embarrassed about being caught. "What? No. He's not my boyfriend yet. Yeah, I was thinking about him." she admitted, a hint of shyness marring her face.

Her reply made Ben even more furious. Why was she thinking about the other guy when he was laying here, in front of her in all his glory? Did she find him boring? No. How could that be? Girls from their college competed with each other just to talk to him. And here he was, offering her his most sought-after company, expecting nothing in return. Yet, all her thoughts were stuck on that one guy, whom he hated with all his guts. Forget about all the philosophical thoughts he had earlier. He'd kill the guy with his bare hands if he were to return Apoorva's feelings. He sat up with all kinds of thoughts running through his mind.

"Ben." he heard Apoorva call. He wanted to yell at her and tell her that he loved her like no other. That no guy would ever love her the way he did. Ben was about to ask a rude 'what'. He intended to do that.

But when he looked up at her angelic face, smiling down at him with so much hope shining in her hazel eyes, he swallowed any rude comments that threatened to spill from the tip of his tongue. Rather, he asked in a soft tone that held nothing but unadulterated love in it. "What is it, Apoorva?" His question brought a full-blown smile to her face, her pearly whites on full display. Then, right there, all of Ben's anger evaporated into nothingness, with all his murderous thoughts flying out of his mind.

"I still have a coffee pending on your account. I want to claim it now. Now that Jeff's not here, this treat will not make a dent in your pocket. I will just stick with a normal coffee." she said cheerfully. Ben stood up from the ground, dusting his clothes, and led her to the cafeteria. In a secluded corner, a table was free. Ben led her to the table and went to get their orders. A few minutes later, he came back with her coffee and his black tea and sat across from her. An uncomfortable silence hung over them, as they sipped their drinks, eyeing each other secretly.

"So, why claim your treat in such a hurry? Did your professor give you more headaches than you expected?" Ben asked, putting an end to the silence. Her face broke into a peal of full-blown laughter at his comment. She set her coffee cup on the table and said, "The headaches he gives me on a daily basis are now a part of my routine," she said, tapping her fingers on the table. "But that is not my reason for having this coffee now." Her eyes darted to Ben's face as she analysed his reaction. His forehead creased, not understanding what she was getting at. She took a deep breath and asked, "Do you have any plans today? After class?"

"Huh?" Ben deadpanned, not understanding her meaning.

"Must I repeat myself?" she asked, annoyance clear in her voice. "It took me so much time to muster the courage to ask you this much. It'll take me even longer to ask again. If you heard me the first time, give me an answer. Otherwise, just leave it," she said, her hand reaching out for her coffee cup.

A ray of hope bubbled in his chest. What if she was asking him out? What if he was the guy she liked? Why didn't he think of it that way? Of course, *it is him that* Apoorva liked. Who in this whole world could resist his undeniable charms? Ben's cocky self was coming into play in his mind. He could wait no longer. What if he lost his chance to be with her just because he was basking in his own glory and took too long to answer her? Ben looked at Apoorva. She was waiting for his answer. Impatience was getting the best out of her as she tapped both her hands on the table.

"I have no plans after class," he said, his voice squeaky. "What? Why did you ask?" He asked in an attempt to get more out of her.

"I have dance practise today. As the art's day is nearing, practise sessions will be longer. So, it'll be late when I leave the auditorium. Could you drop me off at my place after that? If it's not an inconvenience, you could come in and watch the rehearsal." she said, tucking a strand of hair behind her ear.

Ben's heart was screaming with joy at her words. She was giving him a chance to get close to her. What else could that mean? She likes him. Not some other guy. Moreover, she invited him to watch her dance. Will she do that with just a friend? He guessed no. She definitely will not ask a friend to drop her off at home late at night. Now, he was sure that he held a special place in her heart. A place that he has been dreaming so long to occupy. His thoughts earlier were all murderous. He wanted to beat the shit out of the guy Apoorva liked. Knowing that the guy was him made him feel like a clown. What kind of a shithead was he to assume the worst? He didn't know. Yet, it gave him immense relief and pleasure that the guy was him. If not, what would he have done if Apoorva spent her time happily with some other guy in his college? Watching them get comfortable around each other sure would have been torture. His face broke into a huge grin.

"It's not at all an inconvenience. It'd be a pleasure to watch you dance and drop you back home. I'll be there in the auditorium first thing after the last bell to watch you dance. Then, once you are done, I'll take you back home. This is in no way an inconvenience." Ben rambled, not sure what to say.

Apoorva smiled, happy with the way things turned out. If what Ben said was true, doesn't it mean that he likes to spend time with her? She hoped so. She wanted Ben to return her feelings. And she considered this her first leap closer to him.

After she left the cafeteria, reminding him once again of their plan after class, her hands were clammy from all the sweat she shed. Ben was in the cafeteria, looking out of the window and smiling at everyone passing by. He was waiting impatiently for the last bell to ring. Never had he watched Apoorva dance before. His heart was already making mental images of her dancing gracefully on a dimly lit stage, looking like the angel she was.

When the last bell rang, he stuffed his books into the bag hastily and swung the bag over his shoulder. He was about to rush out of the class when he heard Jeff calling after him. He stopped and turned towards his friend. "Where are you going?" Jeff asked, confusion evident on his face.

"To the auditorium," Ben said, smiling like a fool.

"Auditorium?" yelled Jeff. "You should rush to the football ground. Not auditorium." Jeff said, rolling his eyes.

"I know, yarr. I know those finals are around the corner. But Apoorva asked me to drop her off at home after her practise session today. I promise I'll join you guys from tomorrow onwards. No excuses. Please, man!!!!" Ben pleaded.

Jeff relented, understanding Ben's eagerness.

"Tomorrow, Ben. Tomorrow. I want you on the field. I don't care if you have a limp or a lost leg. Do you get that?" Jeff asked, as Ben nodded frantically.

"I won't fail you, buddy," Ben yelled, as he took off towards the auditorium.

He sat in the middle row to watch her dance. After a few minutes, she entered the stage with her friends. They started dancing, with Apoorva taking the lead and guiding her friends personally. Apoorva looked like a goddess on stage. Her movements were graceful, like a ribbon flowing effortlessly in the wind. Every movement of hers was a sight to behold. Time went by, with Ben's eyes fixated only on Apoorva. Once she was done, she collected her things and ran up to him, smiling.

"Bored?" she asked him, his hands deep in his pockets. Mirroring her smile, he shook his head no, making her smile wider.

"You told me that you had no artistic bones in your body. But what I witnessed just now was an artist through and through. A talented one at that. Care to explain?" He asked, feeling baffled.

Apoorva smiled shyly, tucking her hair behind her ear. "I have always loved to dance, though not publicly. I love to dance behind closed doors, where I can dance to the tunes of my heart. It somehow frees my soul, giving me an odd sense of freedom. I never intended to dance for an audience. My friends coerced me into it. Now that I've started to dance in front of others, I feel like I've denied myself this pleasure for too long. I love this." she said, looking passionate in her stance.

"Let me go and change. Then, you can drop me back home, okay?" she asked, making him nod yes.

She skipped excitedly towards the dressing room as Ben smiled at her retreating self. Ben waited patiently for her to return. Even after 15 minutes, when there was no trace of her, he walked in the direction of the dressing room. As he neared the room, he could hear her cries echoing through the corridor. From a short distance, he could see Apoorva clutching her bag to her chest. Before her stood a guy, who towered over her.

"What happened to your saviour, Ben? Call him. He was the one who hit me in the cafeteria. Now you'll pay for the embarrassment he caused me." Ben heard the guy shout. He knew that voice. It was Febin's. He could see tears streaming down Apoorva's face as she shivered in Febin's presence. Her lips were trembling as she clutched her bag closer to her chest in an attempt to safeguard herself. Febin's back was facing him, and Apoorva was yet to notice him in the corridor.

Ben started running towards them as his footsteps echoed across the corridor. Febin turned back to see Ben approaching him with a fist. One swing of Ben's hand, and he was down on the floor writhing in pain. Ben was no longer the calm guy that Apoorva always saw him as. He was livid, and Apoorva was surprised by this face of his.

Ben was beating Febin with no remorse. His punches were strong, cracking Febin's bones sickeningly. His sharp blows made noises that made Apoorva cower. She ran to him and pulled him back from attacking Febin. The look in his eyes was murderous as he said, "Look her way again, and I shall kill you. This is not an empty threat, Feb."

When he turned back, he saw Apoorva, who was crying her eyes out. He held her close, caressing her hair in an attempt to calm her. "Don't worry. It's over. He'll never come near you again," he said, making her nod her head. He caged her face in his hands and looked into her tear-stricken eyes. Holding her close, he whispered sweet nothings into her ear as she sobbed into his shoulder. When her sobs started dying down, he pulled his handkerchief out and wiped her tears. When she calmed down, they walked out of the auditorium, his hand holding her close.

Both walked to their destination hand in hand, uncaring of the rest of the world. Apoorva has not voiced her feelings to him. Yet he knew in his heart that she liked him more than just a friend. Apoorva was now more certain about her feelings for Ben. Nobody had ever looked after her like that in her entire life. Sure, she had her friends and parents. To her parents, she was a duty that they took upon themselves. Being an adopted kid, she was never cared for after Annie arrived in their family. She was side-lined as blood relations got in the way. Her friends had a life of their own. They joked and talked about anything and everything under the sun. But they had their own priorities. Ben was the only person who put her before anything or anybody else. And she knew that her place in his heart was no longer just as a friend.

They strode forward, basking in each other's attention. A cold wind rushed past them, making Apoorva shiver. Their clasped hands shook lightly at the reaction. Ben stopped and unlinked his hand from hers. Unbuttoning his jacket, he placed it around her as she watched him with admiration. "There you go. What kind of a man I would be if I let you suffer while I enjoy the warmth?" he asked, humour evident in his voice.

"You didn't have to," she said, searching for any sort of discomfort in his face.

"My lady." he started, "I am a tough man. It'd take more than a few cold breezes to bring me down." Apoorva laughed at that wholeheartedly as Ben watched the beauty in front of him with awe.

Hand in hand, they once again resumed their stroll, feeling content in each other's presence.

Immersed in thoughts of their own, they didn't notice that they had reached Apoorva's home. Ben hesitantly took his hand out of hers, pushing her towards the gate.

"Guess it's time to say goodbye," Ben said, feeling sadness envelope him. Apoorva turned around to face him and said, "Thank you for today, Ben. I can never repay you for your help. If Febin had succeeded in his attempts today, I don't know what I'd have done. Thank you so much," she smiled, with tears in her eyes.

He stretched his hand to place a comfortable hold on her. She smiled sadly through her tears and looked down at his hands to see blood seeping through his index finger. She wiped away her tears to have a better look at his hand. Feeling her eyes on his wound, Ben tried to pull his hand back in an attempt to hide it from her eyes. Apoorva held on tightly as she examined the wound by bringing it closer to her face. "You are bleeding," she said matter-of-factly. He smiled, trying to hide his embarrassment. "When you get into fistfights, you ought to expect things like these," he said sheepishly. She looked at him pointedly and tore a piece of cloth from her scarf. Taking his hand in hers, she tied it around his wrist carefully, making sure not to hurt him. "Here you are. Make sure to change this dressing once you get home. I did that just to stop the bleeding," she said, smiling sadly at him. "Okay doctor," he mocked, making her smile spread wider.

"Good night," she mumbled with a light smile.

"Good night," he replied, shaking his head lightly. Hesitantly, he turned around to leave, his thoughts never straying from her.

However, he was too content to depart. Apoorva felt safe in his presence. If not, she wouldn't have asked him to accompany her home late at night. He turned around and returned her smile with a grin of his own. "I'd never let anyone hurt you as long as I am alive, Apoorva. Trust me, this is no bluff," he said sincerely.

Ben took a few steps towards her out of caution, testing the waters. He was not sure how she would react to what he was going to do. Yet his heart refused to pull him back. Slowly, he held her close, pressing a kiss to her forehead. Her eyes closed, savouring the sweet moment in all its fullness. With that, he pushed her towards the gate in an attempt to send her home. He left the place once he was sure that she was inside the house, safe and secure.

When he reached his home, his phone beeped, indicating a text from Apoorva. It read, "I have something to tell you on the last day of our college. Please wait for me." Ben smiled to himself, feeling content. That night, he went to bed with a satisfied smile on his face.

At home, as the kitchen rolled in a rhythmic fashion, Apoorva was nonchalant; only the sizzling and chopping could be heard over the joyous humming she was unconsciously focused on, giving warmth to an otherwise ordinary household. It was a usual scene in their kitchen. After a long day, all three women in the family would cook together, while the old man occasionally lent a hand. Fresh vegetables were always available, especially because of the mother's fixation on growing them herself in the yard. Soon, the lovely scent of spices filled the kitchen, and the mother held out a spoon for Apoorva to taste the curry, making the youngest one mumble *favouritism* under her breath. Appu moaned upon tasting the rich flavour and held up her thumb, showing her appreciation, though her mother had already detected her ecstasy by the hiss of her tongue. Apoorva set the table and filled four glasses with water. The incidents of the day were too overwhelming to recall in detail, although the lingering sensation still sat somewhere in the back of her mind, and she couldn't help but wonder if her feelings would be reciprocated.

The next few days passed by in a rush. Preparation for final exams, unfinished dissertations, and the course viva kept them busy, with them barely seeing each other. On the last day of college, Ben sat under the peepal tree, which was now his favourite spot on the campus. College life was coming to an end. Years passed by without any of them realising it. He was fortunate enough to have great friends and find love, though Apoorva didn't know. He knew that he would treasure those memories forever. No matter how successful he became, he was sure to treasure those memories for life.

He could see Apoorva heading his way from afar. He was sure that she'd confess her feelings today and he waited impatiently for that moment.

As Apoorva walked to Ben, she was thinking about the talk she had with her friends that morning.

"Does Ben know that you have been crushing on him since childhood?" Niha asked, making Apoorva shake her head no. She looked more like a child whose candy had been snatched from her hands.

"Girl.... Ben's a rare catch. It's not every day you get guys like him around, and that too single. If you don't act fast, some other chic will take him away. And you'll sit here, growing old, watching them celebrate their life together." Emma said, relentlessly chewing gum.

Apoorva made a dirty face at Emma, who looked like she couldn't care less.

"Really Appu. You won't be able to put up with the grief if it ends up like Emma said. Do something. You've been in love with him secretly for years now. It'd be difficult to cope with the grief if somebody else was to take him away from you." Sminu said, with worry clear in her tone.

"Go Appu. He'd be sitting under the peepal tree. That's his usual spot. This is your last chance." Niha said, pushing her out of her seat.

She stood before Ben, ready to come clean with her intentions. "So, Ben." she started. "Today is our last day in this college. How does it feel?" she asked, making him smile.

"Did you ask me to wait for you so that you could ask me this? But, to answer your question, I am going to miss this campus. I'll always miss our beautiful campus, teachers, and friends. Especially Jeff and..... you," he said, looking into her eyes.

Apoorva smiled at his words. She didn't want some other girl to come and snatch him away from her. She was too selfish to let that happen. She wanted him all to herself, however childish that sounded.

"So?" Ben continued. "Why did you ask me to wait for you?" he asked, trying to get her to speak.

Apoorva closed her eyes and took a deep breath. "I hope what I am going to say will not harm our friendship in any way," she said, making him nod yes. "I have liked you since my childhood, Ben. You were always that guy who seemed perfect in every sense yet was so humble. That fondness for you grew beyond just admiration to love during our college days. I don't know how this started or how these thoughts came into my mind, but I love you. I feel strong and safe in your presence, which I have never felt in anybody else's presence. For the past few days, I have been struggling to tell you this. Then today, since this is our last day in college, I realised that if I let this chance slip, I'd regret it for the rest of my life. I am so sorry if this is something you didn't expect or want." she said, eyeing him warily.

Ben smiled. A genuine, full-blown smile. Apoorva's words were everything he wanted. Closing his eyes in happiness, he simply said, "I love you too." Apoorva's tensed face split into a huge grin, tears running down her cheeks. She wiped them feverishly as she watched him stand up. He wiped her tears with his hands, and gazed straight into the hazel pools of hers, saying, and "I love you too." She cried some more into his chest with happiness.

Ben and Apoorva were now together on a journey that they had both embarked on alone, even before they realised it themselves.

Like two love birds in unison,

As playful as the one that allies them-

She touched his soul as he holds her close

They feel their heartbeats rhyme.

In her eyes shone desire as

There was passion in the air.

Reflection in her look made his heart pound further,

They stood beneath the evening Rayleigh-

Two lovers are set to disappear.

PART 4

Our quest for happiness is everlasting; it never ends, and the hunt only shifts from one thing to another. Some find it in money, some in fame, and a few in love. And when they do, there begins the hustle to sustain it, to not let it go, to acquire more. And with happiness comes the fear of losing it, of being left behind, and of being broke. People like me belong to the last category. For me, love is the food for one's soul; it is my battlefield and my lifeblood. A man who lacks love in his life is a starving man. His appetite never subsides. His thirst for happiness never ceases. Even in pain, the twinge of happiness it imparts is more therapeutic than anything else. Acknowledging the emotion and rolling with it is the best path to eternal delight. Some cherish this feeling beyond any treasure, and some find contentment in toying with it. Our definition of love defines us, the depth of our soul, and the meaning of our life.

Persistent knocks on the door pulled me out of my slumber. Groggily, I stood up from my bed and opened the door to find a very bouncy and fresh April. She pushed past me into the room to drop a garment bag on my bed.

"I've been knocking for quite some time. What were you doing?" She turned to me and asked, plopping down on the bed.

"Sorry," I said sheepishly. "Sleeping on an unfamiliar bed does that to me. I tossed and turned around the entire night. I didn't get a blink of sleep until 5 in the morning." I said, scratching my head.

"Too bad," she said, pulling me down to the bed. I lost my balance and fell on top of her, as her giggles filled the room with gleeful vibrance.

Her lips traced my cheek, awakening pleasurable sensations as every ounce of sleep left my system. I sank further into her, relishing in the wetness of her lips, waking into a ravishing reality. Her hands traced the expanse of my shoulders, treading to the position of my heart, resting there. Her eyes fixed me in place as they danced with hidden mirth. My emotions were all over the place when she said,

"Aren't you a little too excited today?"

Her question brought me out of the bewitching charm her eyes spun. "What?" I asked like a fool.

"Well, your heart is beating like crazy, and something rigid is poking my thigh. So, I was asking, If this isn't a bit too much for a beautiful sunny morning," she asked, followed by a loud giggle. A burst of laughter came from me as I said, "Not my fault. It's all you. Why did you have to look so beautiful in the beginning? You can't blame a man for desiring something this beautiful." I said, making her squeal.

"What? Just a giggle? I praised you this much, yet no kisses for me." I asked, earning a swat from her.

"Morning breath, mister. I don't want to faint," she said, pushing me off her. She stood up, straightening her clothes, and pointed at the bag on the bed. "I picked those shirts for you. Choose any and come downstairs quickly. We are going out today." I took the bag and opened it to see two shirts. A grey button-down shirt and a denim polo shirt. "Not bad, Princess," I commented as I felt the material under my fingers.

"I know, I am the best," she said cheekily and dashed out of the room.

I suddenly felt empty without her in my thoughts. My days without her were filled with agony and longing. After listening to Ben pour his heart out, it felt as if someone added fuel to the fire inside me. It began eating me away little by little until I could no longer hold it in. Once, I tried to imagine myself at Ben's place. The mere thought pushed me off the cliff of longing I was clinging to, scarring me in ways I never thought would be possible. Now, even when those thoughts are several miles away from my mind, they still scare me to no end. Ben's experience made me cherish April and my moments with her even more. I got out of the cobweb of my thoughts, grabbed my phone, and walked out of the room.

When I got down, she served me breakfast. Once done, we scrambled out of the house to buy some time for ourselves alone, away from prying eyes. We visited markets, did some window shopping, and ate almost every kind of street food that the city offered. By the end of the day, I felt like a giant with all the food in my tummy. Bingeing and roaming around were slowly starting to catch up with me, yet April's energy knew no bounds, skipping from one stall to another as if she had all the time in the world. Wherever she went, she dragged me along with her hand, never leaving mine. By evening, I was ready to head back home when she led us to a lake. The place was away from the buzz of the city, deserted, and spelled calm. The lake was flowing silently, with a rhythm of its own. Trees stood proudly on either side, shielding it from the eyes of outsiders, preserving it's tranquilly, and extending a soulful warmth. We strolled along the bank, holding hands, watching the setting sun, and sharing our thoughts and dreams.

"I just noticed something," she said, as my eyebrows rose in question.

"Your ears are so small. Fit for a teenager." The laughter that accompanied her comment was contagious.

She yanked her hand from mine and said, "Catch me if you can." She took off, expecting me to chase her. Two steps into the chase, she stopped, as if some invisible force had pulled her back.

"What happened?" With concern in my voice, I inquired. It wasn't usual for her to stop like that. Was she hurt? Or did she lose something? My thoughts were already on the run.

She looked down and pointed to her feet. My eyes went to her feet, only for my worries to break out into roars of laughter.

"What? "Your girl accidentally stepped in cow dung, and you are laughing like a maniac," she asked, as I again doubled up with laughter.

"I am sorry. But your feet look fabulous now, don't you think?" I teased her, a warm feeling spreading across my chest at her contorted face.

"What shall I do now? If I keep walking like this, it will mess up my dress." Her face was filled with disgust and worry.

I couldn't resist the urge to pull on her cheeks. So, I did just that. I reached out and pulled both of her cheeks. Annoyance marred her beautiful space as she swatted my hand away. "It's not funny," she said, making me laugh.

"Come on. I've got an idea. I'll give you a piggyback ride to the lake. You can wash it off there, alright?" I asked as she let out a sigh.

"Are you sure?" she asked, eyeing me with suspicion.

I bent down as she climbed on my back. "You are so heavy. How much do you weigh? 100kg?" I asked, earning a hit on my head.

"Ha!! Now, I am fat! I felt bad for making you do this. Now, I don't feel an ounce of pity." She said this, making me chuckle.

"Who said love is sweet?" I mumbled sarcastically to myself, earning another hit.

While she washed the dirt off her feet, I couldn't help but wonder about the woman in front of me. Living with a man like me wouldn't be easy for a girl with her personality. I was quiet and broody, while she was the synonym of outspoken and bubbly. I never imagined myself being here with her, not even in my wildest dreams. My heart took its own decisions, leaving me powerless and totally at her mercy. Loving her never came with a choice. Rather, it was an undeniable fact that I tried to fight for so long. Now, looking back, I only have regrets about the time I spent sparring with my heart. No matter what, I was happy for myself—for me losing the war and giving my heart to her. We sat down on the grass, cracking jokes, sharing dreams, and giving playful nudges. The time we spent there was everything I had ever hoped for. We were having a moment of our own, away from nosy glares, surrounded by the chirps of birds and ripples of the lake. This was a space of our own, where we could spend hours without care, laugh without restraints, and finally be lost in ourselves. I watched her, feeling content with her laughter and playfulness. With me, she was never out of spirit. Even in our darkest hours, she would keep her composure and smile as if nothing could ever go wrong. She was my light, my ray of sunshine, my hope, and my life. She reads me like an open book and has the best techniques to calm me and reign in my emotions. She moulds me in unexpected ways, smoothing my rough edges, softening my hard patches, and strengthening my soul with caresses. This was her special place, where she found solace away from the chaos that life offered. She escapes to this lakeside to find peace, stop, think, and contemplate when life becomes hard. April carried herself with an elegance like no other and held down the fort on her own. She had her shortcomings and weaknesses, but despair was not one of them. So, I kissed her, the goddess of my dreams, as I poured my gratitude, love, and longing into the intimate gesture, a simple acknowledgement of her efforts and love.

I sat back, watching the lake flow by, as April sat silently by my side. Never have I felt so content and so rich. It was like having the long-awaited spring right beside me. I still do not understand how I landed this girl or how lucky I was to call her mine. My love for her grew stronger every day, making even the thought of losing her unbearable. Did the stars cross? Maybe.

My thoughts halted upon hearing Roshan call out for us. He jogged towards us, a wide smile plastered on his face.

"What? Planning to jump in?" He asked, sitting down next to me.

"In your dreams," mumbled April, making me chuckle.

"You guys are no fun," said Roshan, making me pull April closer. His face contorted into a look of disgust, making me laugh.

"What?" I asked. "We are still young. Long way to go before hitting rock bottom. Right, darling?" I asked, wiggling my eyebrows at April.

"Yeah. So now, off you go. We don't want you to steal our precious time together." Said April, shooing him away.

"Touché. I am hurt, sister." Roshan said, placing a hand over his heart.

"Hey!!! I have an idea." April said, suddenly more excited than ever.

"Oh no. If she is that excited, some trouble is definitely cooking in that pea-sized brain of hers," Roshan said, eyeing April with suspicion and apprehension.

I turned my head towards her, raising my eyebrows in question.

"Let's go on a bike ride." "A long, romantic one," she said, making me smile and Roshan jump.

"But how? We don't have a bike handy." I asked, playing along.

"Of course, we have one. Don't we, Roshan?" she asked, smiling mischievously at him.

"Hell, no. I am not handing my baby over to you lovesick puppies. Nada. Nah," he said, shaking his head vigorously.

"Okay. Fine. Then I am going to tell Auntie about your late-night hangouts. Come on, Ashiq. Let's go home." she said, pulling me away.

"What? No. You can't do that." Roshan exclaimed, making us stop.

"So, keys?" I asked, extending my hand. April laughed silently behind me as Roshan pulled his keys out and handed them to me.

"Bye, brother. Take a taxi back home. You are so sweet," said April, making cute faces at him.

The Devil in disguise." I heard him mumble, making me smile.

We mounted the bike and took off. Her hands wrapped around my torso, making the hairs on my body stand up. Feeling the wind on my face and her body pressing against mine was my newfound euphoria.

Water drops fell on us as her grip on me became tighter.

"Don't stop. Let's just let go. Feel the rain; enjoy this time together." She breathed into my neck, causing my emotions to run wild. I rode away, with no particular destination for that wonderful journey, to the horizon.

The feeling of riding, with no real destination in mind and her arms wrapped around me, was otherworldly. The fresh air, the melody of her whispers, and the intimacy that the moment granted made me want to get trapped in it forever. Nothing she said was new. They were the same old dreams that we had repeated in words and thoughts a million times. Sauntering through the same territory again, holding her hand, only made those dreams brighter, never to be dimmed forever. Her words depicted the life I so badly wanted to live. And I knew that with her by my side, I'd never be tired, even if I had to live the same life over and over again. With her, I never felt tired. Maybe that is the effect that love has on people. You never grow tired of that one person around whom your entire life revolves. We have had our fair share of quarrels in the short time we have known each other. None of those disagreements ever made me want to let go of her. Rather, they bound me more to her. Every time we quarrelled, another knot made its way into the beautiful mess we called our bond, strengthening it to the point where it hurt physically to stay away from her. The last few days, when she was not there with me, were the loneliest days of my life. I didn't know how to start my days without her sweet voice yelling at me to wake up or to end them without the chaste kiss she used to leave on my forehead. Having missed everything about her for the past few days and going crazy over her memories, I cherished every moment of this ride with everything in me. The boundless joy of experiencing the freedom of being myself, with no veil shadowing my true self, was back in my soul, bringing down the flames of agony roaring in me. By the time we decided to go back, my mind was calm and at peace like a child's.

When we reached home that day, it was too late. Almost all the lights were out, and we were both dripping wet. Her mother was waiting for us on the porch and rushed to us as the bike came to a stop. Pushing April aside and throwing a towel in her way, she started drying my hair while April whined about her uncaring mother. We both parted ways at the foot of the stairs. I went to my room, changed my clothes, and took a warm shower. When I was done, I went to the balcony to continue my favourite pastime, stargazing. April walked into the room silently, brushing her long, wet hair. She was about to take a seat across from me when I pulled her into me and whispered, "Always be by my side. It is us against the world." I saw her eyes swell up with overwhelming emotions as she shook her head, trying to clear her head. She snuggled into my arms, feeling the chilly breeze, extending warmth and care.

"My piece of heaven," I whispered into her hair, placing a kiss on top of her head. My arms pulled her further close, breathing in her scent and relishing in the warm act. This was my salvation, the endpoint of my worries, and the escape from my sorrows.

The night passed, giving way to a beautiful, sunny morning. I heard a knock on my door. I tried getting up, but it was hot all over. My back was sore, and I had a splitting headache. Unable to get up from the bed, I called out, "Come in. The door is open." April came in, looking fresh and bright.

"What happened?" "Why aren't you up yet?" she asked, making me smile.

"I am feeling sore all over, and my head is aching," I said, as her smiling face morphed into one of worry.

She came close to me and placed the back of her hand on my forehead.

"Oh my god!!! You are burning up. You have a fever. Why didn't you call me? I thought you were sleeping in, considering we got home late." she said, as she fussed over me. She rushed to the walk-in closet and came out with a box of medications. Pouring a glass of water from the jug, she extended a pill and the glass to me.

"Drink up," she commanded, making me smile.

"Yes, madam," I said, mocking a salute. A few minutes later, she helped me lay back on the bed and went down to get me something to eat. She returned with a bowl of vegetable soup and forced me to drink it all. Once done, she started placing a wet cloth on my forehead to alleviate the fever. That day, she never left my side and sat by my side on the bed even while I was sleeping out of exhaustion. She took care of me and fed me like a brother, admonishing me for not finishing my food or taking my medicine. Three times during the day, she brought me herbal tea, wiped my body, and changed my clothes.

"We are never getting soaked again." "Never, ever," she said for the hundredth time, making me sigh.

"Hey, forget it. I'm feeling much better now." I said, hoping to relieve her stress.

"It's decided. "We are never going out in the rain again," she said, effectively stopping me.

At night, she went downstairs again to get us food. I was feeling so well, so after she left, I got out of bed and went down. She was in the kitchen, cooking something. Her mother met me in the hall and felt my temperature. "How are you feeling, son?" She asked me warmly.

"Much better. April was so attentive. It's all her effort," I said and sat down on the couch.

After almost an hour of waiting, April came out of the kitchen. Her eyes widened with joy upon seeing me. "When did you come down? How are you feeling now?" She asked, feeling my forehead with the back of her hand, and started fussing over me.

"Hey, hey, calm down. I came down an hour ago, and I am all patched up. I don't feel a headache, nor is my back sore. My fever is gone, and I'm as good as new." I said, pulling her down with me. "I missed a whole day with you, thanks to this damned fever. I need some time with you now that I am going back soon." I said, feeling heavy at just the thought of parting with her.

"What? An hour ago? Why didn't you call me?" she asked.

"An hour just flew by. Any relative of yours who passed the hallway in the last hour came to me and asked me about my fever and all. So, I didn't feel your need. Now that nobody is here, I need you. Stay with me, please." I said, earning a smack from her.

"A few minutes more. I'll be back in, say, 20 minutes. But right now, I am preparing something for us. Tonight's dinner is about us. Me and you, alone, in our own space, away from the questioning gazes of others. Okay?" she asked, making me nod. Placing a chaste kiss on my forehead, she rushed to the kitchen to stop the food on the burner from burning. I threw my head back as I waited for her to get done with her cooking, desperately waiting for her proximity as I felt sorrow grip my heart at the thought of leaving her here. I am a selfish man. I just cannot take her away from her family and ask her to come with me. But the man in me needed her like the air I breathe. "Twenty minutes more," I mumbled to myself in an attempt to keep calm.

True to her words, she came back to me in 20 minutes. though those were the longest 20 minutes of my life. She led me to the balcony, which was decorated with string lights, plush carpets, and colourful pillows. Five casseroles containing food sat in the middle of the carpet. We sat on the carpet, enjoying the proximity and munching the delicious food she had made. Everything was made according to my taste, and I moaned every time a morsel hit my taste buds. It was overwhelming to see her care for me so much while I didn't offer anything in return. She cares for me like no other, loving me without expecting anything in return. I gazed into her expressive eyes, finding nothing but unadulterated joy in them.

"Hey. I've got something for you. I don't know if you'd like it." She said this apprehensively, tucking a strand of hair behind her ears.

"I don't think that I can dislike anything that you get me," I said, caressing her hands with mine.

She took out a black velvet box and extended it to me, like a child. I opened it to find an Audemars Piguet watch with a black rubber-coated strap. I looked at her, my mouth hanging wide. The look of apprehension on her face made me open and close my mouth like a fish out of water. She raised her eyebrow slightly, waiting for me to say something.

"How could you even think that I'd dislike something like this?" This is an 'over the top' gift. I said as I gave it to her, "Tie it around my wrist." Her eyes glistened with unshed tears as she clutched them around my wrist.

"It's nothing. You deserve more. I can never pay you back for all that you're doing for me," she whispered, as tears fell down her cheeks.

"I don't expect you to," I said, claiming her lips. They tasted sweet, addicting, and soft as I deepened the kiss. A moment later, she pulled away, pushing me away, and said, "Someone will see us. I will not get caught for making out in public." Her words made me laugh, as her cheeks blushed with a deep shade of red. I sat back, leaning over the pillows, and pulled her into my chest as we both lay there, gazing at the stars.

Our love is like an ocean, too deep to fathom.

You and I are on a voyage, two sailors far from being lost.

The magic that's cast, upon us it stays,

Unsure of the waves or the path it paves.

My soul craving for yours, like the sail, does for the wind,

Holding our hands, we sail beyond what's known.

We were both wrapped in a blanket, gazing at stars, while munching on the chocolates in our hands. April shifted slightly in my arms to face me. "What happened to them, then? Febin is an asshole. But are they happy?" She asked, eager to know more. I caressed her hair as I shifted my gaze to her face.

"Well, he was stirring up unnecessary troubles. So Ben handled him the way people like him should be handled. I initially intended to keep this away from you. Now that you are this curious, I can't keep this away from you." I stroked her cheek.

"What?" she asked, a curious look crossing her face.

Apoorva, in her usual way, took to the task with energy and passion. When focused, she always stuck her tongue out, just a little, and moved it around as she worked. Half an hour later, there were two identical lines, perfectly straight, of the same thickness, and exactly 4 inches apart, going from one end of the hall to the other.

By now Ben was all up, wondering what she was going to do—how could this make any sense in light of the "surprise" she was planning for her own birthday? Funny enough, these sorts of theatrics were not rare. She did it many times in the past, though he could never predict why. It didn't matter if he or her sister understood her intentions. She was always excited and had new ideas every year. She always said that they'd understand her if they had a brain. Their brains never worked as she expected, so they held their tongues and waited for her to finish. These were the times when Ben would sit in a corner and watch her like a hawk. If somebody noticed the looks he gave her, he will get a good beating for the creepiness that wafted off him. Ben always wondered: Having her as his partner to walk through the different stages of life was a fortune that rained on him without asking. And he would forever remain a slave to that love with no complaints. His thoughts were clouded by her, the haze surrounding him like a dream from which he never wanted to wake up.

After what seemed like an eternity of sighing and eye-rolling from Annie, his little ball of mischief jumped off the table and prepared to leave.

"Lo there! I'm done!" exclaimed Appu, throwing her hands in the air and sending Ben a look that he couldn't completely decipher. But the part of the look that made sense told him: "Escape if you want to." Little did she know, Ben couldn't leave to save his life! He was 'enchanted', as Annie would mock.

The entire day went by with Ben watching Apoorva finish up all her theatrics for her birthday, which would be the very next day. Ben had plans too, but he wasn't sure where to fit them with all the grandeur Apoorva was preparing for herself. The day was all about Annie rolling her eyes, Apoorva snapping back, and Ben trying to figure out what he had gotten himself into. The girl was so consumed by the idea she was bringing to life that Ben doubted if he could ever say no to her antics. It was around 9 when Ben finally kissed her good night and left.

"Any big 'surprises' for me, Mister?" Apoorva hit send as she jumped onto her bed.

"Well, nothing as big as the one you're throwing for yourself," Ben texted back from the siege of his pillows.

"I'm sorry I got a little carried away," she typed away, adding a smiley at the end.

"Oh? "So madam knows?" he wondered to himself, smiling at the screen like a lunatic.

"Well, in my defence, it's my birthday!" came her reply, with the emoji of a dancing girl following it.

"That's your defence?" Pretty weak if you ask me." He added an angry face to his message.

"Sorry naa, I'll make up for it tomorrow," came her reply with a sad emoji.

"It's okay, silly! I was only playing around," he said, and leaned back, hoping to find a more comfortable position. He sent emojis back and forth, spamming her inbox with his overflowing emotions. No message came back, even after ten minutes, making him conclude that she was fast asleep.

"You had a long day today. Good night." He hit send and went to sleep.

The next morning, Ben went to pick up a few things he had ordered for Apoorva. And from there, he had to go check with the florist too, from where he'd be picking up some flowers in the evening. It seemed like 24 hours were not enough. He called Apoorva a couple of times, and like him, she too was busy for the day. It's only a birthday! Ben thought to himself. What wouldn't he do to keep that silly girl of his happy? Cheesy thoughts invaded his mind as he waited impatiently for the evening. Apoorva's friends were also planning something. They were very secretive and refused to let Ben know about their plans.

On the other side, Apoorva was in the hall downstairs, overseeing everything. Her fingers moved across her mobile screen constantly, jumping between the pins on Pinterest.

She was taking the whole house and time for herself, as everyone else had gone out to get something or other. Holding a planner in one hand and a pencil in the other to check the list, she stood in the middle of the room, slowly spinning on one leg and observing the room, eyeing everything cautiously. As time passed, her nerves were a mess, leaving her sweating like crazy. Apoorva had no idea what Ben would be planning or what he would be getting her, but she loved the anticipation. Her fingers traced the lining of the planner she was holding, tracing the patterns on its cover. She flipped through its pages and shook her head as if to get something off her mind. Idiot! She mumbled under her breath.

The doorbell rang, waking her from her daydream and bringing her back to reality.

Ben is here already? Apoorva yelped. If it were Mom or Annie, they would have just walked in. And besides, there would be that familiar screeching of tyres if it were them. But Ben had said that he wouldn't be here for another hour, she thought. So is this his big surprise? She could already feel her cheeks getting heated. She was sure that a tinge of red was coating her cheeks. She fixed her dress in haste and skipped towards the door. She took a deep breath and pulled the door open with a wide grin that she couldn't stop from spreading.

"Oh, hi," the happy grin on her face faded. The beautiful grin was now replaced by a forced smile.

"Happy Birthday, Apoorva," the guy said with a smile that wasn't quite there, "I know I am not welcome here."

"You remembered?" she asked, surprise clear in her voice. "Oh, thank you, sorry, I didn't expect you, so-" she fumbled, trying to find words.

"That's alright," Febin cut her off, shooing away her embarrassment with his hand. "So, what's going on?" He asked, as his eyes pointed towards boxes huddled up inside.

"Nothing, it's just that it's my birthday. I was arranging som,tuff... You know... Birthday... So..." Apoorva said, shrugging her shoulders.

"Yeah, sure, fine!" said Febin in a retreating manner. "You must be expecting people, and that's my cue to leave." He turned to leave.

"Oh no, wait, how silly of me! Why don't you come inside? I'll get you a drink maybe." She couldn't let him go, even if she didn't like his presence even a bit. "I'm a little blown away by this whole party thing, you know..." she said, not knowing what else to say.

"Yeah, sure...   "If you insist," Febin slowly walked in, carefully studying the drawing room.

The room was huge. With the white and coffee-brown-themed furniture complementing the pastel beige walls, it looked as if something were in the works. Unpacked cartons lie in the corner, tape torn and papers falling out of them. Apoorva's phone lay on the couch, and he noticed its little green light blinking. Febin followed her across the room, where she showed him her preparations for the party. He just nodded, barely listening to her gleeful rant.

"Why don't you have a seat? I know it's a little bit of a mess, but I can get you a drink, of course," Apoorva politely said, pointing to the sofa.

"Yeah, sure. I'll wait here then," Febin said, with a withheld sigh.

"Just a second," Apoorva gestured in an apologising manner, and she rushed to the kitchen, wiping her forehead as if she were wiping off the awkwardness. "Why is he here? What is he doing here? Is it only me who's finding it awkward? Why do I feel something is not quite right? I should call Mom. No, she'll worry. It's stupid. Should I call Ben? I should call Niha. Where's my phone? Shit, I must have left it on the table. No, couch. I don't know. What should I do? Should I do something? No, no, no, I'm overreacting. He doesn't feel anything at all. Let bygones be bygones. College is over, and so are all those petty affairs. It's over. He's over it. I'm over it. Probably the girls are over it too. No, no, no, it's stupid to go and pick up the phone to check if they're really over it. It's your birthday, Apoorva! Stop being a child for once!" Her head was filled with a thousand thoughts at once; she felt it would explode. It was odd for her to have Febin over, especially after all that fuss in college. So, she decided to get him a drink and not make his stay any longer than needed.

"I'm so sorry to keep you waiting," she called out from the kitchen as she carried the drink, only to find no one waiting for her anywhere. She placed the tray on the table and walked to the drawing room to see if Febin was there. But he wasn't. Strange. She thought to herself.

"You there?" Nobody answered. Is he really gone? Weird. She didn't understand. The door was wide open. "Maybe he just left," she mused to herself. She turned around and saw her phone lying on the couch.

The notification of an incoming message made her take it. "I'll be there in 10," said Ben. Relieved, she unlocked the phone and texted back, "Be here soon."

Apoorva was still in awe of what had just happened. Why did he just vanish like that? She was only away for a moment. She surmised that maybe it was awkward for him too. Then why did he come over in the first place? Odd. She thought of calling him. Later, she decided not to. "It'd only make things more awkward," she thought to herself. But, no matter what, she couldn't shake off the uneasy feeling his visit left behind. "Why did that guy have to be so weird? Just why? Shut up, Apoorva. You are weird. Shush, now get back to work." She chastised herself, forcing her mind to concentrate on her happiness.

Just then, she heard a car pulling onto the porch. This time, she was startled beyond normal. "What if it is Febin, again?" She rushed to the door to not let him in when she saw Ben coming out of the driver's seat. "It is Ben only," she reassured herself in an attempt to calm her raging heart. He walked around the car and pulled open the passenger seat to get the flowers, along with two huge shopping bags. With both his hands full, he kicked the door shut and tried to wave at her.

"Hey, girl!"

"Hey, baby," sighed Apoorva, her shoulders down and her head tilted to the right.

"What are you making that face for?" Ben asked, "Should I be worried?"

"No, it's nothing," she dismissed him and rushed forward. "Here, let me help you with that," she said, pointing at the bags he was carrying.

She considered telling Ben about Febin but decided against it. It seemed so bizarre and silly that she brushed it off, thinking that it was not important. Also, she was too eager for the evening to let anything else assume the main stage. After carefully placing all the bags on the table, Apoorva turned to see Ben settling on the couch.

"You need a drink?" she asked.

"So, this isn't for me?" Ben asked, pointing at the drink she had made for Febin.

Her face fell, not knowing what to tell him.

"Hey, was anyone here?" he asked, noticing the look on her face.

"Wait, there's something..." Apoorva said, sitting beside him.

"Febin was here?" asked Ben.

"How do you know?" She raised her brows.

"Well, I just saw him outside while I drove in."

"You saw him?" she exclaimed, her eyes widening.

"Yeah, I did." Why?" Ben didn't understand why she was getting so worked up about it.

"Well, he was here," said Apoorva, her eyes still wide.

"And..." he prompted her to continue.

"And then he disappeared. She didn't know how to explain to him the whole situation.

"Disappeared?" Ben asked, not understanding her point.

"Yeah, I just left to make a drink for him, and he wasn't there." she said, her eyes scrunching at the thought.

"...," Ben said nothing.

"He just vanished," she said, as if trying to make sense of her words to herself.

"He left without a word?" Ben asked again.

"Yeah, he left without saying a word. It was strange to have him over, but it became stranger when he left." She turned to him, trying to make sense of Febin's actions.

"I never really liked that guy, you know..." Ben admitted. The fear of something going wrong was starting to build in his chest.

"Me neither... He gives me the creeps," she said, lying back on the couch.

As Ben and Apoorva were brooding over the entire incident, her mom and Annie returned, their hands full of bags. Annie was carrying the cake from the baker, while her mom carried the pastries. "Apoorva," her mom called out from the porch.

That was the third surprise of the day for her. "Coming, Mom," she answered the call and ran outside, Ben following her footsteps.

Ben helped them carry all the stuff inside and arrange it on the table. Just when they were done with everything, her friends came, carrying numerous bags. The house became alive again with Annie and Apoorva taunting each other, their mom yelling at them both, Ben laughing his ass off, and the girls chasing each other. Among the merriment, they almost forgot about Febin and his sudden drop-in. The happiness was so contagious that the impending strike of bad luck was not anticipated in the least.

| PART 5

December is the month of lights, snow, and feasts. The chilly blanket of snow envelops all—joy and sorrow alike. It brings with it the sweet impatience of waiting and slight pain of loss, the relief of letting go, and the apprehension of the impending. For lovers, it is time to look forward, make new memories, and make life more beautiful.

Childhood is what we miss the most yet are unable to get back to. I had neighbours who'd let their goats graze the fields with no one to guide them. By dawn, they all return to their owners on their own. Love is like that. Letting go will help it find its way back to us. Time is what it deserves, and time is what we should provide.

Ben was in his room watching the rain pour down, blessing the earth with the elixir. The dim light rays entered his room, bathing the interior in a warm coral glow. His room was a mess, and he intended to fix that. The huge pile on the table was where he would start. He moved to his table and reached for his diary. His diary was the only thing that had a proper spot on his table. Not a day of his life went by without him making a diary entry. The routine was something that caught up with him from the time he started writing without mistakes. More than any photographs or videos, he preferred reading his diary whenever he wanted to relive certain special moments. Photographs could only give a reflection of what was on the outside. His diary entries were the most detailed reflection of his emotions. Every one of them, written down without losing the depth of it. A piece of paper fell. His hands reached out to grab it. Leaning against the wall, basking in the warmth of the sunlight, he opened the letter.

Hey Ben,

I won't start with the cliché questions. Your girl is a bit different like that. She loves being real. Did you smile today? Yup, you read me right. Smile? I guess that question brought a smile to your face. Well, that was my intention.

We couldn't speak yesterday. But I know that a few moments of separation will not kill our love for each other. Whenever I am sad, I think of you. You know why? Because I know you'll love me no matter what happens or what others say. That being said , I still miss you. I miss hearing your voice, I miss your warmth, and I miss everything about you. Hey, I am entitled to feel that way. Come to me as soon as possible. I feel incomplete without you.

Well, that's enough mushiness for a day. Let me tell you something. Having a younger sibling is double trouble. We wrestle, and she beats me black and blue. Your girl is no less beautiful, but I am the elder one. Fighting back is often not a choice because I am the older one. Though she's very irritating, I love her so much. I wouldn't even change a hair on her head if I could.

Now what? I have talked about you, my family, and... Yup, likes and dislikes. I am a huge fan of Brazil. Yes, man!!!! I am talking about football. What? Only boys can watch football? We girls too can. Why should boys have all the fun? But it's such a pity that you like Portugal more. Believe me, Brazil is far, far better. I am absolutely, madly, and deeply in love with Casemiro and Neymar. You'll love them too when you start watching them in action.

Here I am, spewing nonsense to you through a letter, and you, reading it, are smiling like an idiot. No matter what others say, this feels good. I can talk to you with no filters on. I can be myself with you. This is what I've always craved. For someone to talk to without having to hide anything. See? I am being emotional now. I told you, this is not going to be a cliché love letter.

Why do you love me so much, Ben? You know what? Don't answer that question. I want you to keep me close like this for the rest of our lives. I will follow you to the end of the world, no questions asked. Just stay like this, smiling, forever. Because my smiles start from yours.

Yours, and only yours,

Apoorva.

Ben folded the paper and kept it safely inside his drawer. Thinking about Apoorva always brought an unending smile to his face. His girl was the best, regardless of all her shortcomings. The trust and understanding they had for each other were like no other relationship. His thoughts were scattered elsewhere as his hands did the job at hand, moving across the table and arranging the pile of books and papers. His phone vibrated in his pocket, pulling him out of his thoughts. He took it out to see Apoorva's name flashing on the screen.

Hey, mate," he chirped through the phone.

"Hey Ben, what are you doing? Did I disturb you?" Apoorva's sweet voice chimed from the other end.

"You did. You did disturb me big time. I was reading a letter from my girl. Your call stopped me from reading her heartwarming words." Ben said his speech was more serious than ever.

"Did I? Well, you can talk to the sender directly. Why read a letter when you can talk one-on-one?" Apoorva asked, realising the tease in his words.

"Reading a letter and talking over the phone are two different things. It's good that I can talk to you whenever I want, but reading your letter makes me realise the depth of the feelings we have for each other. Ben said, his voice reflecting the emotions he kept bottled up in him.

"True. I'm so in debt that it sometimes scares me. What if...???" She dragged on, unable to say more.

"What if what?" Ben asked, his concern thickening his tone.

"It's nothing. I tend to overthink. Let's enjoy this very moment. Why think about the future now?" she said, trying to divert the topic.

"It is not nothing, Appu. If we start keeping things from each other, what's the basis of our relationship? We are in this together. You are my comrade. We support each other. We don't keep things from each other. Now, tell me. What were you going to say?" Ben said, his eyes narrowing as if Apoorva could see him.

"Ben... please don't get mad with me. I... I told you, I tend to overthink." Apoorva blabbed, getting fidgety with every passing moment.

"Will you stop with these introductions? Just tell me what you were going to say," he said firmly.

"What if, on one fine day, you suddenly feel that I'm not good for you anymore? What if you find someone more beautiful and smarter?" Apoorva asked, as her eyes brimmed with unshed tears.

"Where did these thoughts come from? Appu, I promise you. I won't find you lacking in any way. Not in this life. You are my girl. In my eyes, no other girl is more beautiful or smarter than you. You make me the happiest man on earth. You don't have to feel insecure. What makes you believe that, Apoorva?Do you doubt me?" Ben asked, concern etching his voice.

"It's not you. It's me. I will never doubt your love for me, Ben. I just..." Apoorva said as tears rolled down her face and her voice became thick with emotions.

"What is it, Apoorva? You can tell me anything. You know that, right?" Ben asked, his tone comforting.

"I will tell you something, okay? But please promise me that you'll not think any less of me after knowing this. I can't bear you doing that to me." she said, unable to hide any longer.

"I promise you. Nothing can change the way I think of you. I love you, Apoorva. As long as you understand the meaning of those words, I don't think you need any other assurance from me." Ben said, killing every apprehension she had.

"Ben..... I'm.... I'm adopted. They didn't have kids at that time. After trying so hard, when the gods didn't smile at them, they adopted me. But when I was 5, Annie was born. Their own flesh and blood And then they lost interest in me. I can't blame them for giving more importance to Annie. Who'd want an orphan who knows neither of her parents when they have a kid of their own? But it still hurts. Knowing the reason for their disdain doesn't make it any better. I know I am being ungrateful. I have no right to feel so; If not for them, I'd sleep on the streets with no one to look after me. But I still want to feel like I belong.And I don't feel it with them. I'm so messed up. Now, I am messing it all up with you." She sobbed uncontrollably.

Now, my girl, you listen, and you listen carefully. You'll never mess with me. I know that. You can never do that. And, about your family. We all crave love, Appu. We can never be happy without the warmth that feeling extends. It's not your fault. It's in our nature. If they are ignoring you for Annie, it is their fault. When people adopt, it's not only the law that binds them to the child. They are promising a life filled with warmth and love for the child, not just material things. If your parents are unable to do justice to that promise of theirs, it's their fault. You have me, Appu. I'll always love you, no matter what. You'll always be my first priority, even before myself. Now, I want you to wipe those tears that I know are rolling down your cheeks. Actually, tears make you look uglier." Ben joked, making Apoorva laugh.

"See, this is the Apoorva I want to see every day. The happy girl who loves me more than anything in the world." Ben said as Apoorva smiled through the phone.

"Just keep in mind that every tear of yours is a stab to my heart. I promise you, with me, you'll never have a dull moment in life." Ben said, his voice thick with emotion.

"I know. I just... it just got out of hand," she happily said.

"Now off you go, my lady. Because we both have projects to complete.And make sure to wear that smile from now on." Ben said, making her laugh.

"As you say, my lord, I love you." Apoorva said, playing along.

"I love you too," Ben replied, smiling on his own. Hanging up the phone, he returned to the task of arranging his room and his thoughts, never straying from Apoorva.

Mornings are the blooms of hope, filled with the chirps of birds and warm sun rays. Apoorva finished her cereal in one sitting and went inside her room, locking the door behind her. She opened her wardrobe and pulled out her clothes one by one.

"Nothing looks good on me. Why do I have such dull clothes?" she murmured to herself. Anything she tried looked either like a second skin or a bean bag on her. Finally, after trials that lasted over an hour, she settled on a long pink top with white embroidery and black leggings.

Excited to show her choice of outfit to her mom and sister, she skipped downstairs to see them chatting in the kitchen.

"Mom, how's this?" She called out from the entrance of the kitchen.

"You'll look good in anything, Appu," her mom replied, stirring the curry in the pot.

Oh, mom, you're being too generous. Just now I tried on everything in my wardrobe, yet this was the only one that seemed to look good on me." Apoorva said, making Annie laugh.

"That's because you chose it on your own. Normally, it's mom or dad who chooses clothes for you. You are too lazy to even do that." Annie said, making faces at her sister.

"That's not it. Nothing suits me. I look like a potato in a sack." Apoorva said, frowning to herself.

"Appu, believe me. You look great in whatever you wear," her mom said, focusing on the task at hand.

"Okay. Okay. Now, I need your help," she said, making her mom turn.

"What?" she asked, looking at her daughter.

"What should I gift him?" "I can't decide on anything," she said, narrowing her eyes at her mom.

"He is an athlete. Buy him a pair of running shoes. Why is it so hard?" her mom questioned, raising an eyebrow at Apoorva.

Apoorva's eyes darted to Annie, who nodded at her.

"Then its decided. I will buy him a pair of running shoes. Thank you, people." Apoorva chirped happily and ran upstairs.

Life was not easy for Ben and Apoorva. Forget about meeting each other; they didn't even have much time to talk to each other over a phone call. But today, they have decided to make up for all those lost times. Apoorva was so excited that her plans knew no bounds. Surprises and gifts were a must for her if she and Ben were to meet after such a long time. But her idea of gifting never came with what exactly she would give Ben. And there, her mom and Annie came in handy. They suggested every sort of gift she can buy Ben; the list never seemed to end. After loads and loads of suggestions, she concluded that it could not be something trivial. It should be something Ben can use or carry with him all the time. That's how she zeroed in on the idea of sports shoes. She knew that he had been eyeing it for a long time. But the price tag stopped him from taking it home. So she decided to go to the mall with Niha, who wanted to go on a shopping spree for herself.

That day, she got ready and walked out of the house to see her mother opening the car door. She skipped towards her in an attempt to appease mom into dropping her at the mall.

Mom," she called out, making Grace look up, her eyebrows creasing. "Drop me at the mall, please," Apoorva urged, trying her best to seem cute. Grace's eyebrows shot up, making Apoorva's smile turn a bit wider.

"Get in," she said, closing the door behind her. Apoorva ran up to the car and secured herself with the seat belt in the passenger seat, closing the door after her. Silence enveloped them as they drove out of the porch, the mellow tune of Mohammed Rafi's melody filling the car. Apoorva was staring out at the passing vehicles and trees on the roadsides when Grace started talking.

"So, why are you going to the mall now? Weren't you supposed to meet Ben today?" Apoorva's eyes turned towards her mom, who never took her eyes off the road.

"I am meeting him today, mom," she assured. "But Niha needs to buy some stuff from the mall for her cousin's engagement. So, while she gets her goodies, I'll be buying Ben's gift," she continued, looking ahead of her.

"Is everything fine between you and Ben? You guys are meeting after a long time!" her mom asked, a teasing tone entering her voice.

Apoorva never hid anything from Grace. Her mom was the one person who knew her inside out and never judged her for anything.

"Yaa, mom, all well. We are just busy with our work," replied Apoorva, smiling widely at her mom as if to prove her point.

"Don't lose each other in this rush. At the end of the day, more than any position or money, it is the love you have for each other that matters." Her mom stated that the teasing tone had now been replaced with a serious note.

"We are trying, mom. It is not easy, but we won't give up." Apoorva stated, staring ahead of her.

The mood in the car shifted; the melody of the song was long forgotten. Grace was no longer smiling, her expression turning solemn. Apoorva knew that her mom was serious and needed her to assure her of the same.

"Believe me, mom! We will work this out. If only we could get rid of those deadlines." Apoorva said in a frustrated tone.

Her mother tried to calm her by playing her favourite song. Seeing her child juggling with too many emotions, Grace could no longer show the fret on her face. Her face relaxed, shooting a warm, understanding smile at Apoorva. Seeing her mom calm, warmth enveloped her, washing away all her worries.

The rest of the ride went by with them chattering about everything under the sun. When they reached the mall, Niha was already waiting for Apoorva at the entrance. Grace was about to get down to greet Niha, but the honking of the trailing cars stopped her.

"No need, mom," Apoorva said, understanding her mom's dilemma. "You can meet her some other time. Thanks for the ride." She waved at her mom, who drove away after her approval.

"Let's go in," Niha said, breaking her out of her trance. They both walked into the mall, cracking silly jokes.

Apoorva was looking around, her gaze stopping at nothing particular, when Niha tapped on her shoulder. Her face was dead serious, making Apoorva's expression turn solemn as well.

"What happened?" Apoorva asked.

"I need to ask you something, Apoorva. Please don't get me wrong," she replied. Apoorva was now on her toes, bracing herself for the impact.

"You know you can ask me anything, right? Please go ahead. You are scaring me now." Apoorva spoke, her face heavy with worry.

"What..." Niha trailed behind, her gaze seeking Apoorva's. Seeing her friend nod in encouragement, she asked, "What do Alexander the Great and Winnie the Pooh have in common?" Apoorva's face went from worried to horrified to confused in an instant. Niha could no longer hold it in. She cracked a laugh, making Apoorva look at her in disgust. She lifted her hand, smacking Apoorva on her back. "You and your jokes! I was scared to death," she spat out and walked away. Niha jogged behind her, annoying her further. "Come on, yaar. I don't know the answer. Please tell me. Please, please, please." Apoorva turned to see her friend looking at her with puppy eyes. Her anger-filled façade broke away, causing both girls to laugh out loud. By the time their laughing spree was over, they had reached their destination.

Apoorva was always a stranger to the luxuries of life. She was adopted, which always made her dad's least favourite. His hostility towards her was evident from the day Annie came into the world. Little Apoorva was oblivious to his sentiments; grown-up Apoorva was not! So she stopped asking him for anything. Be it love or money. But her heart was always yearning for love. The duel between heart and mind went on, with the mind losing every time.

So, while Niha decided to go for the best pieces, despite them being expensive, Apoorva surfed around for discounted items. She went in and out of different stores, her eyes searching for boards announcing discounts. Finally, after almost two hours, they were both done. Niha had both her hands full, while Apoorva clutched onto the one bag that was her gift for Ben. By the time they finished, both of them were starving. So Niha pulled Apoorva to the café, where they ordered burgers, fries, and iced tea. Apoorva finished her portion in one sitting. It was getting late, and she couldn't let Niha stay and enjoy her food for long. So she dragged her away from the café while she munched away on her fries, having no care of the world. Their day out ended with them clicking pictures at the artificial waterfall at the entrance of the mall. The day was well spent, but their chit-chats were still unfinished. Both girls were overjoyed, and Appu seemed relieved and at ease after her demanding schedule. They separated with a loving hug and took different paths home. As soon as everything was finished, Apoorva began seeking a taxi while Niha went downstairs to her car.

Apoorva hailed a cab and arrived at the park where she and Ben agreed to meet. She was already fifteen minutes late when she arrived at the park.

She strolled into the park and took a look around. He was leaning against a tree when she saw him there. He opened his arms to encircle her as she jogged in his direction. She sighed in relief as she sank into his arms, their breaths blending.

"You look beautiful," he breathed out, enjoying her warmth.

"Thank you. I brought you something," she took out a box and gave it to him. "Open it," she said, as Ben started unpacking it.

"Wow... running shoes. I've been eyeing this for quite some time. Thank you so much!" he exclaimed, pinching her cheeks.

"Now, I brought you something too," he said, taking a lilac-coloured box with a purple ribbon tied around it.

She eagerly pulled the wrapping paper apart to reveal a pencil drawing of theirs, both of them smiling into each other's eyes.

"How is it? Did you like it?" Ben asked, apprehension marring his voice.

Apoorva pulled her gaze from the picture and looked into his eyes. Her eyes were wide as a myriad of emotions flashed through them. "Like?" she asked. Ben's forehead creased, his hands reaching out to the photo frame, trying to take it from her hands. Apoorva pulled the frame closer to her, hugging it to her chest like a kid. "I loved it, Ben. You couldn't have chosen a better gift for me," she said, as she smiled through the tears brimming in her eyes.

"You scared me. When I saw your expression, I thought, I did some mistake by getting you this." Ben said, wiping her cheeks with his kerchief.

Apoorva laughed through her tears, shaking her head vehemently. "I could never dislike anything you get for me, Ben. But this may seem trivial to you. But for me, this is the best gift I could ever get." she said, as his thumb traced her cheek and his eyes looked deep into her soul.

Ben took hold of her hand and walked forward, enjoying the dim rays of the sun and the warmth of the trees. Lightning struck and thunder rang violently above them, making Apoorva clutch his hands in a tight grip.

"Scared?" Ben asked, looking down at Apoorva, who was tucked to his side like a scared puppy. She shook her head in disbelief, her gaze fixed on the looming clouds above them.

"It may rain..." It started raining before Ben could complete his words. It soaked them both, their clothes sticking to their bodies. "Soon." He said, looking at Apoorva, who was giggling like a kid. He held her hand and ran under an oak tree, hoping to get shelter from the heavy rain.

"You are soaked. We should get a cab and go home. You may catch a fever if we stay here like this." Ben said, reaching for his phone.

Apoorva stopped him, holding his hand, shaking her head no. "No," she said. "We are supposed to enjoy this, Ben. In this overly chaotic world, this is our little moment, away from prying eyes and judgmental words. We can have it all for ourselves, just for us, forgetting every worry and pain, so far away from rights and wrongs."

Something primal stirred in him, making him hold her close. She smiled, looking as demure as ever, her hands wrapped around his torso. He leaned forward, his eyes seeking permission, and hers closed, silently proclaiming the desire to be mutual. Their lips met and moved in sync, feeling each other with rough abandon. Above them, the thunder once again clapped loudly, making Apoorva snuggle more into his chest. He held her close, a sense of serenity spreading in his chest. "You are safe with me," he murmured softly into her ear, making her smile. "I will hold on to that," she replied. The clouds cleared the sky, ending their lone time together. They held each other's hands and walked out of the park, reminiscing about the beautiful memory. Bidding bye with a promise to meet again, they went to their respective houses, wishing for time to fly faster.

Reaching home, Ben took a long shower to relieve himself of the fatigue of the day. Just as he got out of the shower, he heard his phone ring. He looked at the screen to see Jeff's name flashing on it.

Hey, bro," came Jeff's voice as soon as he picked up the call.

"What?" Ben asked, bored out of his mind.

"Let's go to Q-Max," Jeff said, making him sigh.

"Q-Max? What yaar? I came back just now. What I need right now is good sleep." Ben said, yawning.

"I knew you'd give me that excuse," Jeff said. "But think it over. There's a flat 50% off sale going on. It happens only once a year. The joggers that you were eyeing from last summer are on sale too." Jeff said, trying to tempt him.

"Okay okay. I'll meet you at the store in 15." Ben said, cutting the call.

As promised, Ben reached the store to see Jeff waiting for him.

"You just need to see the word discount to start shopping. Why are you so girly?" Ben asked, feigning disinterest.

"Ha!!!! Look who's talking. The biggest miser of the century If you were not interested, why did you come? You could've stayed at home watching Masha and the bear in your bed. I didn't force you to come. I just asked if you were interested. And shopping is not a girl's monopoly. We too need to shop. And if I am a girl, then those who associate with me so closely must also be girls. So what are you? Girly or boyey?" Jeff asked, pointing his finger at Ben.

"Boyey? Is that even a word, you knucklehead? Say something that is acceptable to the human race." Ben said, looking at his friend weirdly.

"Well, in my dictionary, if girly is a word, then boyey too is a word. Why should girls have all the fun?" Jeff asked and turned around, walking away from Ben. Ben caught up with his friend with a short jog and knocked his head with his hand, causing Jeff to yell "Abuser." All eyes in the shop turned towards them for a second. Unaware of the attention they drew, the duo walked forward as if nothing were wrong.

Ben and Jeff browsed through the clothes and tried a few. By the time they reached the cash counter, they both had a huge pile of clothes in their hands. Suddenly, his phone rang, flashing Apoorva's name on the screen.

With greater difficulty, he picked up the phone, balancing it between his head and shoulder.

Hello, baby girl," he said through the phone.

"Hey, handsome. Where are you?" She chimed from the other hand.

"I am at Q-max with Jeff," he said, balancing the clothes in one hand and holding the phone with the other. "Why did you call?" he asked.

"What? Now I can't even call you." Apoorva asked, feigning to be sad.

"Hey. "I didn't say that," said Ben, turning defensive.

"Hey, I was just teasing you. I called you to tell you that Annie got me a piano. Well, technically, she asked Dad to get me a piano. All the same. Dad would never get me something on his own. But that's not our point. Tell me when you get home. I'm so excited to play for you." She spoke from the other end.

"Yup. Now I am also excited to hear you play," he said, feeling confused by her words. Why wouldn't her dad get her something on his own? Did he dislike Apoorva? Was it even possible for someone to dislike her? He did not believe it. Apoorva was an angel. Disliking her would be a sin.

"Oye. Hello. Ben... Where are you?" Apoorva's voice came from the other end, breaking him out of his reverie.

"Yes. Yes. I am here. Just zoned out. So I'll call you when I reach home, okay?" He said, hoping to ask her about her cryptic words some other time.

"Okay. "Bye," she said.

"Bye," he said, hanging up the call.

Ben reached home late that night. His father was on the patio, reading a newspaper.

"Hey dad!" Ben called out, inviting his dad's attention.

"Son"! his dad exclaimed, making Ben smile. "How was your day?" he asked, making Ben nod his head and say, "Good, as always."

Dad folded the newspaper, kept it aside, and took off his glasses. Ben knew that he had something to share with him. His father wouldn't simply put away his newspaper for nothing.

"Son..." Ben's father started Ben nodded his head as a signal for him to continue.

"We are planning a trip," Dad said, making Ben's face light up like a lighthouse.

"Where to?" he asked, unable to contain his excitement.

"Switzerland," his dad replied, making him even more ecstatic.

"When?" Ben asked, as his dad sighed.

"Next month," he replied, to Bens frown.

"One month, dad? One month? Couldn't you plan the trip after two months?" Ben asked, causing his father to ask "What is the problem with next month?".

Ben shook his head irritably and said, "Dad I have a lot of presentations coming up next month. Now I'd have to hear an earful if I asked for a leave. On top of that, I'd have to prepare the presentations for those who are going to present them instead of me. Double the work, dad. You owe me one for my sufferings, okay?" He said this, causing dad's face to turn funny.

"What?" he asked, baffled by his dad's expression.

"Who asked you to come along?" Dad asked as Ben's mouth hung open.

"Huh?" he deadpanned, unable to voice out his amazement.

"You are not coming along. Me and your mom—my wife—want some time for ourselves. If we tag you along with us, it will not be our time." His dad said, making Ben shoot a wide-eyed look at his dad.

"A trip without me? How could you, dad?" He asked, totally astonished by the revelation.

"You're an adult now. You're earning well. You can go on trips with your friends. Now, let us have some time to ourselves. What's so shocking about it?" His dad asked and stood up.

Ben was stunned and in no hurry to leave him.He stood there, not knowing what to say. His dad was now walking away from him. He stopped near the door and turned again to face Ben.

"I lost track of what I was about to say. Take care of your mom's plants and the house while we are gone. It is a 14-day trip, so don't let her plants wither away. Dusting should be done on alternate days, and the flowers in the flask should be changed twice daily. Make sure not to leave lights and fans on. Oh, yeah, the pipes, too. And, please, if you don't know how to cook, don't burn down the house and order takeout. We would love to see the house still standing when we return home. There's one last request. Don't call your mom every now and then. If there's anything urgent, shoot me a text. We'll call you when we get time." He turned his back to Ben once again and went in, calling out for his wife.

Ben climbed the steps, still not able to digest his dad's words. He dialled Apoorva's number as soon as he stepped into his room. The call was picked up in a ring.

"Hello brother. My sister is currently stationed near her new piano. Do you want to hear her play?" Annie's voice came from the other end.

Ben smiled at Annie's choice of words. "Yes, please," he replied.

"Well, here you are," Annie said through the phone. Ben could hear the faint voice of the piano and Apoorva's voice singing along with it. He listened to her, holding his breath and not missing a note. Her music stirred in him feelings that he didn't know existed and held him captive, unable to shake them out. Once the song was over, Annie handed over the phone to Apoorva, leaving her to talk to him.

"You never told me that you knew how to play the piano," Ben complained over the call.

"Back during my school days, I used to attend classes. But that was long ago. I thought my skill would've gotten rusty over time." She said this, pressing random keys and making odd sounds.

"You are so talented. I wouldn't have known this if your sister didn't get you this piano," he said, amazed at her different sides.

Ben sat there, holding the phone close to his ears, refusing to miss even a beat. That night, Ben went to bed listening to her melody.

Ben sat under the same oak tree, watching over a sleeping Apoorva. She snuggled more into him, making him smile. He caressed her face, moving a few hair strands that fell over her cheeks. He watched her with so much love and a hint of pride, memorising every crease and curve. He bent down and placed a kiss at the base of her neck. With that, her eyes flew open, and her face lit up with a smile as soon as they landed on his. She sat up, blushing profusely, looking around for any watchful eyes. As if nature herself were reliving the memory, rain poured down on them, making Apoorva snuggle closer to him. This was now a routine of theirs. They would meet up under the oak tree, enjoy the rain, and leave the park soaked from head to toe. He held her close, erasing any twinge of fear from her heart and replacing it with the warmth of security. Suddenly, she left his hand and jogged out of the shade of the tree, giggling like a schoolkid. He jogged behind her, trying to catch up when the storm brewed more violently.

The atmosphere became darker as chilly air surrounded them. The wind blew harder, making it difficult for him to jog further. He called out to her but got no response. He made his way further, despite the strong wind, to see a pool of blood near a clearing. Her bracelet was lying in the pool, soaked in the crimson fluid, making Ben breathe heavily. He fell to his knees, sobbing and yelling her name frantically. With a huge roar, he woke up from the dreadful dream to find himself drenched in sweat on his own bed. Reaching the bedside table, he took his phone and checked the time. It was only 3 in the morning. He badly wanted to hear her voice. Yet he restrained himself. He didn't want to disturb her sleep over some stupid dream of his.

The day was uneventful, yet Ben's mind refused to stay calm. The feeling of something looming over him was eating into his insides. It was 5 in the evening, and yet he received no calls or messages from Apoorva. He'd check his phone every now and then, checking for any missed calls from her. His whole day went like that, waiting for her call. By 6, he ran up to the terrace to make a call to Apoorva. He didn't care if she was doing something or if his call would disturb her. He didn't care if she found him annoying. He wanted to feel at ease, to put an end to the gnawing feeling in his chest. He pressed the call button and waited for her to pick up. There was no response from the other end. He tried again and again. At last, on the fifth call, the phone was picked up.

"Where were you? I've been calling for so long. Where were you? You didn't even send me a message during the day." He completed the sentence in a breath, without extending his hand or waiting for a greeting.

"Ben. Ben..." came a different voice from the other end. He frowned, not liking it a bit. "This is Niha," the voice from the other end said, making him sigh.

"Hi, Niha. Where is Appu? She didn't call me the whole day, and now she even refuses to answer my call?" He asked, feeling annoyed.

"Actually, Appu is in the hospital right now. She had difficulty breathing last night, and things got worse by 2 a.m. We had to bring her to the hospital." She said this, making all the alarms in Ben's head flash red.

Ben couldn't breathe for a moment. Apoorva was in the hospital. What went wrong for her to be hospitalised suddenly? Why didn't they inform him? More than anyone present there at that time, he believed that he had a say in her life. "What? How is she? Is she alright? Just wait for me. I'll be there in no time." Ben hollered through the phone. Without waiting for her reply, he cut the call.

Ben clutched the keys in his hands and ran to the parking lot. By the time he got inside the car, strapped himself in, powered the engine, and stepped on the pedal, He was breathing and sweating heavily. His hands were shaking, and his heart was drumming in his chest. For a moment, he gripped the steering wheel hard to keep himself from shaking. Seeing no end to it, he started the vehicle and sped out. He drove forward, honking his horn continuously to clear any hindrance that came his way, wanting to be by her side as soon as possible.

Ben's thoughts were going haywire as he drove to the hospital. She was all right when he last spoke to her. What went wrong after that? No matter how hard he tried, he couldn't find a reason for her breakdown. His hands were clammy as he gripped the steering wheel for dear life. His eyes brimmed with unshed tears as his vision turned blurry. Wiping the tears with the back of his hands, he stepped on the gas pedal, hoping to see her at the earliest.

Ben ran into the hospital building, following Niha's directions. When he reached the floor that she was admitted to, he saw her friends waiting in the corridor. Emma sat on a chair, her eyes closed and her head tilted upwards. Sminu's head rested on Emma's lap, her eyes reflecting their conflicts over the past few hours. Niha stood by the window, gazing at the faraway fields, deep in thought. Ben ran to them, hoping to get a briefing on her condition. Just then, the door to his side opened, and out came a doctor who looked at him with a puzzled expression.

"Apoorva's...?" he asked.

"Fiancée." Ben replied. That broke her friends out of whatever trance they were in. They looked at him with sorrow-filled eyes. Ben averted his eyes from theirs and turned to the doctors.

"What happened to her? Is she alright? Can I take her home?" He asked away, wanting to soothe his racing heart.

"Can you calm down, Mr.?" the doctor looked at him expectantly.

"Benedict, Ben," he replied.

"Mr. Ben, why don't we go and have a chat in my room?" The doctor asked and walked inside, hoping for him to follow.

Ben walked into the room after him and sat down on a chair, his mental exhaustion kicking in. The doctor handed him a glass of water, which he thankfully accepted. Once Ben finished drinking, the doctor sat across from him, the professional façade back in place.

"Ben, there is no point in keeping things from you. So, I am being straightforward here. Apoorva is suffering from arrhythmia. This is a condition when the heartbeat of a person is either too fast or too slow. Apoorva's heartbeats are too slow. This can cause difficulty breathing."

"What...what can we do? Do we have to take her somewhere else? Just tell me what I can do to help her." Ben asked, worry evident in his voice.

"Ben, no doctor is going to prescribe her better treatment than this. Doctors can only prescribe medicines. Physical health and mental well-being are closely related, Ben. Medicines are poison if the patient is not in the right state of mind. I don't know Apoorva personally. But, even after being on medication, if she's having breakdowns like these, you should be careful. Make her happy. Love is the best medicine that mankind has ever known," the doctor said, making Ben nod.

"I think I can do that," Ben whispered, his voice barely audible.

"Now, you can visit her. But don't go in there with that moody face on. Smile. Your worries should not hold you back from your smiles." The doctor stood up, patted his shoulder, and went out, closing the door behind him.

Ben entered Apoorva's room to see her lying on the bed with her eyes fixed on the ceiling. He closed the door behind him and sat down next to her bed on a chair.

"What happened to me?" she asked, her eyes not leaving the ceiling.

"Nothing, Appu. You don't have to worry about anything. Everything's alright," he said, massaging her hand.

"Everything is alright? Then, why am I here? My friends are standing just outside this door. Yet they refuse to come in and meet me. A nurse came in, told me that my friends were waiting outside, but didn't care to brief me about my being there. Finally, you!!!! You came here, smiling from ear to ear, hoping for me to buy that façade. I have known you for years, Ben. I can see right through your lies. That smile of yours is forced. Why are you guys lying to me?" Her words broke into a loud sob as her hand tightened around his.

"Apoorva, don't you believe me?" he asked, brushing her hair back.

Sniffling, she nodded her head yes.

"Then, believe me. There is nothing for you to worry about. Just take care of yourself and take your medicines on time. You'll be alright. I'll make sure of that. Hmm?" he said, making her smile through her tears. She nodded again, pulling him closer so she could rest her head on his chest. Their moment of intimacy was disrupted by a knock on the door.

Apoorva sat back, leaning on the pillows. Ben called out, "Come in." Entered a nurse with a tray in her hands.

Setting the tray on the other side of the bed, she took out a syringe and filled it with medicine. Panicking, Apoorva looked towards Ben with wide, fearful eyes, silently asking him to say no. He winked his eyes at her and started making silly jokes, to which she laughed heartily and forgot her fears. Once the nurse went outside, he asked her, "You just got injected without shedding a tear. Isn't that something worth celebrating?". For the first time that day, Apoorva smiled. A simple, wholehearted, and breathtakingly beautiful smile And it made his worries disappear. Everything was alright. Appu was. Her smile said that. And that mattered the most to him.

Later, her friends came in. They all looked tired and deprived of sleep. But the way they tried to cheer up Apoorva, making weird faces and cracking jokes, warmed his heart. His girl was lucky. She had such loving friends who'd stop at nothing to see a smile of hers. Their chatter, laughter, and playfulness made the bland hospital room lively for a while. That's when he noticed the yawns Niha has been trying to hide for so long.

"Why don't you guys go home and take some rest?" he asked.

"Why? Are you tired of us already?" Sminu asked.

"No. That's not it. You have been here since yesterday. Go home, take some rest, and come back later. I will be here until you come back." Ben spoke calmly.

"And, why would you be staying here?" Apoorva asked, making him turn towards her.

"To take care of you," he said in a duh tone.

"But I have the hospital staff here for that. You go home, freshen up, take some rest, and then come back. I won't go anywhere. Change your slippers!" she laughed, pointing to his feet.

Ben looked down to see his feet clad in two different slippers. One was black, probably his dad's, and the other was blue, his own. He shot an embarrassed smile at Apoorva, who kept a hand over her mouth to stop herself from laughing out loud.

"But..." Ben started.

"No buts. Go drop my friends off at home and come back later," she said, shooing them away.

With no choice left, Ben followed after her friends after shooting one last glance at Apoorva.

During the entire drive, Apoorva's friends chatted non-stop. They wanted to surprise her in the hospital. Since her happiness mattered the most to him, he joined their conversation. By the time they reached Niha's home, everything was decided. After dropping them off at their respective places, Ben went home and took a shower. The idea of a nap was tempting, but not as tempting as spending some time with Apoorva. So he drove back to the hospital without giving it much thought.

Ben stood outside Apoorva's room door and knocked. "Come in," a faint voice called out. Ben entered the room quietly and saw Apoorva on the bed reading a book. She was so engrossed in the book that she didn't look up. He approached her slowly and took the book from her hand. Startled, she sat up on the bed to see him smiling down on her.

"What? Why are you here?" she asked, creasing her forehead.

"I can't stay away from you for long, love." Ben winked, sitting down on the bed.

"Mr. Benedict. You should be at home taking a nap. I am perfectly fine here. People are getting paid for that," she said in an admonishing tone.

"Honey, I couldn't bear to part with you even for an hour. Why would you want the hospital staff to take care of you? I am here. I can do it better." He spoke as if stating the obvious.

Apoorva laughed, throwing her head back. Ben never ceased to amaze her. No matter what the situation they were in, Ben managed to make her smile. Once their laughter subsided, Ben's eyes poured into hers intently. He wrapped his arms around her and brought her closer to him. Placing a soft peck on her forehead, he whispered into her ear, "Never scare me like that again. I can't even stand the thought of losing you, Apoorva. Please don't do this to me again." Tears threatened to fall from his eyes as he vehemently fought the urge. By the time Ben unwrapped his hands around her, she was fast asleep.

The sight that greeted Apoorva's eyes when she opened them was far more colourful than the blandness of hospital walls. Glittering papers and Christmas lights adorned the walls, exuding warmth and happiness. Ben, Niha, Sminu, and Emma were present, busy with the preparations. What surprised her the most was Annie and her mother's presence. Ever since she opened her eyes, her friends and Ben were there. But never her family. Though she refused to give it much thought, it was still gnawing at her insides painfully. Now that Annie and her mom were here, her happiness knew no bounds. All of them were so engrossed in decorating the room that none of them noticed her being awake. Apoorva cleared her throat, drawing their attention towards her. The grins that broke out on their faces when they saw her awake made her feel cherished.

Her mom came forward and sat by her side. Combing her hair with her hand, she asked, "How are you, honey?"

Apoorva closed her eyes in contentment. Those words were exactly what she wanted to hear. Not opening her eyes, she nodded yes.

"I knew it. What could possibly happen to you when Ben's here caring for you like a newborn baby?" She teased, making Apoorva's eyes flutter open.

"Ben?" she asked. "Here I am lying on a hospital bed hooked to god knows what kind of machines and you are complimenting him? Let me remind you. You are my mom, not his." She whined, a sour look appearing on her face. Her friends laughed, while Ben tried his best to hold in his laughter.

"Yeah. You are my daughter. But you didn't take care of yourself. He did. Why shouldn't I compliment him for that?" Her mom retorted.

As they continued teasing and pulling each other's legs, a knock was heard. Sminu opened the door to see Apoorva's doctor waiting outside for her routine follow-up. Hesitantly, she opened the door wide, and the doctor stepped in, taking in the condition of the room.

"Just to remind you all, this is a hospital room. And these kinds of things are not allowed here," he said, darting his eyes from face to face.

The youngsters guiltily looked away.

"Doctor," Apoorva called out tentatively. Once he turned his attention towards her, she continued, "They were just trying to cheer me up. I swear, by the time I leave this hospital, these walls will be back to their spotless canvas nature." The doctor narrowed his eyes at the young woman before him. Apoorva looked around, feeling awkward under his scrutinising eyes. Her friends were sneaking glances at her, asking for mercy. The doctor came forward, checked her vitals, read her reports, and said, "I am allowing this just because her condition got a lot better during the past 24 hours." The youngsters' heads shot up in delight as he continued, "But, that doesn't mean that I support all of them." If the word gets around, every room in this hospital will be like this. And I don't want that. Be more discreet, and by the time I discharge her, I want the walls spotless. Get that?" he asked, a hint of playfulness in his voice.

"Yes sir." Apoorva and her friends shouted together.

"This is a hospital. Try not to make much noise," he said, leaving the room and closing the door behind him.

The moment the door was shut, Apoorva's mom released her breath, which she had been holding for a long time. Apoorva and the others looked at her questioningly.

"What? I was scared, okay?" she said, making another round of laughter erupt in the room.

As soon as the laughter died down, the youngsters let out a shriek of excitement.

"Truth or dare!" Sminu hollered, making others yell in agreement. Their game lasted a while, and happiness was the only emotion that made its way into the room. Apoorva was happy; her hatred for the hospital room she was confined to was slowly melting away.

By the time the doctor came for another round of visits, only Ben and Apoorva were in the room.

"So, how are you feeling, Apoorva?" he asked.

"I am fine, doctor. But I was bored to death. Can you discharge me today?" she asked.

Ben stood by her side, holding her hand. He, too, was bored. But what he hated the most was Apoorva's helpless condition. There, in the hospital bed, she looked frail and pale. She looked vulnerable. He hated the sight the most. He wanted Apoorva to be the playful girl that he has come to love so much.

"Apoorva, I know that this is not easy. But I need you here for at least two more days for observation. After that, if you promise to take care of yourself, I can let you go. Discharging you today is not an option. I hope you understand." He said calmly and turned back to leave the room. Halfway through, he turned to Ben and said, "Ben, please come meet me in my cabin after an hour."

An hour later, Ben found himself standing in front of the doctor's cabin, knocking on the door. His heart was beating wildly in his chest, and he was sweating heavily even in the air-conditioned corridor. When he heard the doctor say to come in, he rushed in and stood before him, feeling more scared than ever.

"Ben, please take a seat," said the doctor.

Ben pulled the chair and sat down. "You look like you've seen a ghost, Ben," the doctor continued, seeing Ben struggling to speak.

"I... doctor, what is it? Why did you call me her? Is she alright?" he asked.

"I won't sugarcoat this, Ben. She's okay. For now. But you have to be more careful now. Never let her be alone. Her medicines should be taken at the right times. and keep her happy. That's all you have to take care of." He finished talking, making Ben nod.

Back in Apoorva's room, Ben saw her looking out of the window. She looked lost. Apoorva was all smiles and lively around her loved ones. Yet, at the rare times when she was alone, she felt something dark looming over her heart. Though her thoughts were unsaid, Ben knew. Ben never needed words to understand her. She did not do so for him. Their relationship was at a place where even a twitch of an eye could be understood by one another. But, given their situation, Ben was unable to do what she wanted now. So he did the best thing he could do. He called Niha and asked her to bring Apoorva's favourite homemade sweet and sour noodles. He had heard Apoorva chatting nonstop about Niha's masterpiece recipe. Apoorva's diet restrictions didn't allow her to take fatty foods like noodles, but Niha assured him that she'd make a healthier version of them for Apoorva. By dinner time, Niha had the noodles delivered to Apoorva's room. As promised, she made it healthier by adding lots of vegetables and using less oil. Ben opened the packet sent by Niha and served it on two different plates. Apoorva, who was sitting on the bed engrossed in some novella, not knowing the food had been delivered, now sat straight on the bed and sniffed the air. "I smell Niha's heavenly noodles," she said, making Ben smile.

"Yep. Niha sent it to me. I have been spending a lot of time in the hospital eating those tasteless soups. So she took mercy on me and brought me her famous noodles," he said, turning to her.

"Only for you? She must have brought enough for me too. Give it to me." Apoorva said her eyes lit up like Christmas night.

"You? You are not allowed to eat these. Your food chart clearly says that you should have leafy vegetable soup tonight. She brought it for me." He said this, making her eyes go wider.

"That's not fair. Let me talk to her. She's my best friend. She should consider me first, before you." Apoorva pulled her phone out and started dialling Niha.

Ben went to her and took the phone from her hands.

"I was just joking, okay? She brought this over specially for you. To suit your dietary routine, she cooked it with less oil and more vegetables. I was just messing with you." Ben said, holding her hands.

Ben brought the plates to Apoorva's bed and gave one to her. He sat across from her on the bed, cross-legged. They chatted and ate the scrumptious meal heartily. The night went by with Apoorva falling asleep in Ben's arms.

Two days later, Apoorva was discharged from the hospital. Ben took her home, where her friends, sister, and mom were waiting for her. The relief of seeing her back home laughing cheerfully was clearly visible on their faces. That night, there was an air of festivity at Apoorva's home. Apoorva was grateful for the efforts they had put in, and she thanked them for it. Niha, Emma, and Sminu stayed back, while Ben went home for the first time in two weeks. Though none of them said anything, worry gnawed their hearts as Apoorva continued to celebrate, thanking the gods for the selfless love she was showered with.

The way her eyes follow him,

The way she feels beside him.

The way her shadow touches his,

The way longs to cuddle him-

If that isn't love, then what is?

They connect through the pathway of souls,

Decorated with winsome flowers,

Their world in sync,

Sings their song

Their romance

For their dance.

Upon reaching home, Ben made every effort to help Apoorva and ensured that she recovered quickly. For this, he started making every effort he could to make his lady happy and stress-free. One day, while at the supermarket, Ben met his best friend, Jeff.

Jeff and Ben were classmates in college and shared a perfect bond. After college, Jeff pursued his dream career and became an Army officer. Both friends were in touch with each other, but they had fewer chances to meet due to Jeff's posting. Ben requested that Jeff come to his place for a few days to cherish their college life again and have some peaceful moments.

He was thrilled and promised his best friend a meeting in the coming week. Ben came home and narrated his encounter with Jeff to Apoorva, and they both were delighted to meet him.

The following Friday, Jeff got a phone call from Ben, who had invited him to dinner tonight. He confirmed his availability and started getting ready for dinner. On the other hand, Ben and Apoorva began making delicious dishes for Jeff, and he made special sandwiches and noodles for him, just the way he liked them during college.

At around 8 p.m., a bell rang, and it was Jeff. Ben was delighted to see his best friend and hugged him tightly. He met Apoorva and asked about her health, as Ben had already told her about the incident. Apoorva said to him that she was fine and was recovering fast. They sat down and began to discuss their college lives and the fun they used to have.

They talked about teachers, classes, lectures, the canteen, and the time they had spent.

"Remember your secret place, Jeff?" Ben questioned.

"Of course, it was a major suspense for most of the time!" Said Apoorva.

Jeff started smiling and asked them if they still remembered the whole scenario, to which everyone nodded yes.

During their college days, Jeff was a strict guy with anger and trust issues. Most of the people in the college didn't like him due to his nature, but Ben knew his tender heart had a soft corner. While they were in college, Ben started noticing that he used to disappear every day at a particular time. He was extremely curious and wanted to know about this mystery. He repeatedly asked his friend, but all his efforts failed since he didn't get any clear answers to his questions.

One day, Ben and Apoorva decided to follow him after college. They were shocked to see the place. It was an orphanage for girls. The girls didn't have any family and considered Jeff their elder brother. Jeff was shocked to see them at the orphanage and greeted them warmly. He narrated an incident where he met a girl lying on the road and crying for help. Since he was small and didn't know what to do, he brought the girl to the orphanage. His frequent visits to the orphanage made him everyone's favourite, and the girls started to consider him their big brother.

Ben and Apoorva were in tears after listening to the story and felt proud of their friend. They started teasing him by saying how lucky he was to have so many sisters and so much love and affection all around. Since then, it has been their daily routine to come to this orphanage and spend time with the children. Also, they used to teach them and bring them food and games to play.

All three were in a deep state of nostalgia and started missing the orphanage and that time.

"Hey! "Let's go again tomorrow," said Apoorva.

Ben and Jeff nodded, and all three were extremely happy and thrilled to visit that place again. That night, no one slept and everyone made plenty of dishes for the children.

All three had dinner and drinks while talking and cherishing the old days. It was extremely late, and hence they asked Jeff to stay there for a night to enjoy himself more.

They started their journey to the orphanage in the morning and took some delicious chocolates, games, notebooks, and other essential things for the girls. Upon reaching the orphanage, all three were extremely happy to see the growth of the orphanage and the progress these girls have made over these years. Most of the girls got educated and are leading their lives confidently. Also, they saw some new little princesses in the orphanage and greeted them with warm hugs, kisses, and gifts.

The orphanage staff recognised them and planned a special meeting with the girls and all the team members. The senior girls greeted them, thanked them for their contribution, and tied Rakhi to Jeff since he was their elder brother. The trio narrated to the girls their office stories, and Jeff told them some incidents from his latest war. The girls were so fascinated and motivated by these incidents that they promised to work hard and get a job to fulfil their dreams and ambitions.

Everyone was thrilled to hear this, and while they were coming back, the girls gave them beautiful gifts as a token of love and affection. A few girls made handmade sweaters for them, while others made paintings, cookies, and chocolates. All the members of the orphanage, including the staff, were highly delighted by the motivation and dedication the girls got from their visit.

While returning home, Jeff, Ben, and Apoorva were pleased and content. They decided to pay a visit every month to ensure that the girls were in an optimal state and inquire about their welfare and health. On the way, they stopped at a street food junction to grab their favourite foods and get a few things packed for dinner.

Life couldn't get any better for Apoorva and Ben. Work was hectic. Their schedules were tightly packed, and they could hardly find time for themselves. The work life was beautiful, yet more than what they had signed up for. At night, they'd share the difficulties with each other over the phone, drifting to sleep without knowing. Any holiday meant bike rides and picnics. One such fine day, while they were riding to the horizon, watching the beautiful sunset, Apoorva said, "Let me drive."

Ben stopped the bike near a tree and asked, "Why? Is the rider in you impatient?" It was no news that she could ride bikes with ease. But it was not often that she asked to drive.

"Yup. I just want to. Please," she said, looking at him with puppy dog eyes.

"Okay, okay," he said, moving back and making space for her to mount the two-wheeler. All geared up, she ignited the engine, making the automobile roar to life. Before pulling off the sideline, she extended a piece of paper towards him. "Keep that with you. Read it when you reach home, okay?" she said, revving the bike forward.

The weather was drizzly, making the road slightly slippery. Ben's arms extended to either side, feeling the cool gush of wind washing over him. Apoorva's joyful laughter reached his ears, cooling his senses as well. The rain got heavier, soaking them both in its wake. Ben let the raindrops grace him, feeling the cold envelope him. His hands tightened around Apoorva's jacket, the heat of their bodies mingling in a strange way. The ride was smooth, with nothing to worry about. Apoorva has always been a careful rider. Her attention would never stray from the road, no matter the circumstances. There was a loud screech of tyres when Apoorva made a quick curve. Apoorva was freed from Ben's control, and his body flew across the street. Ben's eyes began to close on their own before he could realise what was happening. Apoorva's hushed pleas, pleading with him to stay awake, could be heard from a distance. In an effort to locate her somewhere close, his hands scoured the area on either side for her. He attempted to stand up, but the pain was intolerable. To find her, he tried crawling about. Nothing he did seemed to work. It appeared as though his body was shutting down and preventing him from regaining control. Ben attempted to shout out for her, but he was unable to speak. No sound could be heard coming from Ben's throat as he attempted to shout out for her. His eyes were filled with tears as he lay there. What was going on with Apoorva? He was aware that she would have crawled to his side if she had been able to, just as he had attempted to do. But she was nowhere to be seen. Only her cries could be heard. She made sounds as though she was in excruciating pain. What was he to do? If something happened to her, Ben knew that he wouldn't live his life as if nothing had happened. A life without her seemed grey, like the colour had been sucked out of it. Laying there, praying for some kind heart to find them, was his only option. He felt so useless at the moment, as he cursed himself for his fate. As time passed, her cries subsided, leaving only a ringing sound resonating in his ears. Not long after, his eyes were too closed, despite his best efforts to stay conscious.

The next time he opened his eyes, he saw a white ceiling. Different machines surrounded him, with tubes attached to his body. An oxygen mask sat over his nose, easing his intake of breath. Ben looked around, hearing the machines beep. His whole body ached with unimaginable pain, making it impossible to move. He tried to call out for someone, but no sound came out of his mouth. His throat was dried up as if it hadn't seen a drop of water in weeks. Ben lay there, unable to move, waiting for somebody to come in. In what felt like an eternity, a nurse came in, holding a file and pen. Ben looked at her hopefully, wanting to drink some water. The nurse noticed him being awake and smiled.

"You're awake?" Her tone was gentle, soothing his soul.

Ben motioned with his hand for some water to wet his throat.

"Oh, I am sorry," she said, running to get water from the nearby table. She poured a glass of water from the jug and moved towards him. Raising his head slightly using her other hand, she placed the glass to his lips, helping him drink. With great difficulty, he sipped water, a few drops flowing through the sides of his cheeks. Once he stopped sipping, she gently placed his head back on the bed, wiping the water droplets from his cheeks.

"What happened to me?" he asked, his voice rough and strange to his own ears.

The woman smiled sadly, making fear grip his insides.

"Two weeks ago, you were rushed to the casualty department of this hospital with a broken rib, broken limbs, and massive blood loss. With your relative's consent, we conducted some surgeries on you to bring you back to life. After that, you were in a medically induced coma; your body needed time to heal," she finished off, beaming at him.

Though the woman was relieved about his miracle pull-through, his throat was still constricted with fear. She didn't say anything about Apoorva. If they took him to this hospital, they must have found her too, right? Ben's eyes started watering with the thought of them leaving her there. "The girl?" he mumbled. "There was a girl with me. She too was injured. Where is she?" Ben asked, hoping to hear about her well-being. The nurse's face fell, an uncanny expression taking over her features. "I was hoping for you not to ask this question. But now that you have asked, I should tell you. She's no more. When she was brought here, she had a head injury. We did everything we could. Her body was too weak to combat anything big. In the end, she suffered a cardiac arrest. We are sorry, but we couldn't save her." As soon as the words left her mouth, Ben's head fell back, his heart twisting in pain. Apoorva was gone, leaving him alone forever. The realisation hit him hard, turning his world upside down. Even now, he wasn't fit to leave his bed to pay respects to her. His eyes started shedding the tears that he made no effort to keep in, making the nurse leave the room to give him some privacy. Ben lay there, reminiscing about his memories with Apoorva. He wished to go back to the past and undo the tragic events. Hell, if he could, he would've traded his life for Apoorva's.

As he was lying there, thinking of all the alternative possibilities, the nurse once again stepped into the room. She held a piece of paper in her hand, which had smudges of blood over it. She extended it towards him and said, "Here, we got this from your jacket. You would want to read this." Ben had seen that letter earlier. Apoorva placed it in his pocket just before their last ride together. With shivering hands, he took the letter from her hands, mumbling a simple thank you. As more tears poured out of his eyes, the nurse once again left the room, leaving him to his sorrows.

Hey Ben,

I don't know why I am writing letters to you when we could just chat with each other over the phone. Today is the age of technology. Yet here I am, writing letters to you like an old hag stuck in the nineteenth century. But you know what? I'd always prefer letter writing over chatting. I don't know why, but when I write letters, it lets me vent my sorrows in a better way. No chat could ever give the satisfaction and thrill of reading a letter.

I was rambling. Just so that I get the courage to write everything that comes to mind.

By now, you might have understood that my feelings for you are not simple. I didn't know how to tell you this in person. So, I decided to write it all down. I love you, Ben. I have never been so sure about anything else in this world. It feels so good to know that you love me too, equally, if not more. I was a girl who never wished for anything. A life as privileged as this is a blessing for people like me. But now that I have known love from you, I couldn't help but weave dreams and wish for them to become real. All I want is a life with you. See? You've become a part of my life, which no matter what I do, I can't get rid of. The funny thing is, I don't want to get rid of you or our dreams.

You know what Ben? I have spent all my life as a wallflower. A shadow many knew existed but never really noticed. My joys were unshared, my sorrows unheard. You are the first person who has ever valued any of my feelings. Whenever I am happy, you are there to share it with me. Whenever I am sad, you listen to me, expecting nothing in return and giving me a shoulder to cry on. I had lost all hopes for a better life until I met you. Now that those hopes have bloomed again, I just can't let them wither. I don't know what I would do with my life if you left me. Things like these may seem trivial to you. But for me, these are all I've ever wanted.

Now, my life is you, only you. My thoughts, dreams, and wishes revolve around you alone. I just want to spend the rest of my life with you, without caring about anything...

Ben couldn't read any further. He felt as if the world was closing in on him. His breaths became heavy as he struggled to breathe. He was sweating profusely, and his hands were clammy. He tried to shout for help, but nothing came out of his throat. Slowly, dots appeared in his vision as he succumbed to the lullaby of darkness.

Death is often an uninvited guest. It arrives at our doorsteps with no warning signs, catching us off guard. The pain that it leaves behind can drown us in endless pits of sorrow. Apoorva's death pushed him into a darkness that seemed endless. Before all this, he was a carefree guy who had nothing to worry about. Apoorva gave him a purpose for his life, which he badly wanted to achieve. Now, without her, his life felt empty, without purpose. Apoorva somehow imprinted all of his universe, leaving her memories wherever he went. Yet, here, he was unable to move freely as they announced her death to him. Emptiness filled his heart, making him numb. He was no longer the old Ben who lived his life to the fullest. He was a guy who had lost everything that mattered.

After that, Ben went into a shock that no one could pull him back from. He was suffering from PTSD, or so the doctors said. If PTSD meant not letting go of the memory of life slipping away from your hands, yes, he was suffering from PTSD. Friends and relatives visited him and sent their greetings and flowers. But he lay there, refusing to acknowledge anything or anyone. Nothing mattered anymore. He didn't want greetings, flowers, or visits. All his needs revolved around a single person—Apoorva, who was no longer there. With her, his zeal for life was also gone. His mom came in every day. She would sit there for some time, probing him in every possible way to talk. At last, she would cry for some time and leave the room, tired. He wanted to tell her that he was no longer that son of hers who used to argue with her about anything and everything. Jeff would drop by every day, spend some time cracking jokes, and lament how he missed him. In the end, after being tired of his silence, Jeff would leave, not before begging him to go back to his loved ones. The only other frequent visitor besides his mom and Jeff was the nurse, who would come in every now and then to check his vitals, feed him medicines and food, change his clothes, and wipe his body, all the while talking nonstop. None of them cared about how he felt. They all wanted the old Ben back. Never had they thought about the excruciating pain he went through every day without Apoorva. Every day, he wished for everything to be just a dream. When he finally opens his eyes, everything will fall back into place as if nothing ever happened. That is, Apoorva would simply skip into the room, hug him ardently, and say, "I am here, Ben."

Days passed by. One day, Jeff sat by his side, holding his hand.

"Ben," Jeff called. Usually, he would come in, start his chatter, and end it on a sad note. Today was different. Jeff was not his usual cheery self. Ben ignored his call to look at him and kept his head turned.

"Ben, look at me." This time, Jeff's voice was sterner, forcing him to look his way.

Jeff stared deep into his soul, a painful expression taking over his features.

"Ben," he started. "I know it must be hard. Life is hard, Ben. Here, people come and go. It's a part of our lives. That is life. I want you back, buddy. No, I don't expect you to act like everything is normal. I know that it is not easy. But, give us something to hold on to, just so we know that you are here with us." By the end of his speech, his eyes were brimming with tears. Ben lay there, emotionless, watching his friend finally leave the room, sobbing like a child.

That night, Ben couldn't sleep. He was not ready to accept life, as Jeff said. He looked out of the window, trying to calm his raging thoughts. A soft palm brushed his cheeks, and he turned to the other side to see Apoorva. There she stood, her long, wavy hair slicked back into a smooth braid. She wore a light pink dress and had a bright smile on her face. He lay there, motionless and tongue-tied, unable to process anything. Her hands slid into his, the feel of her palm making his thoughts come alive. Though her lips traced a smile, her eyes were solemn. Ben's eyes started shedding tears, wetting his cheeks. "Apoorva?" he called out. "Baby, are you really here?" he asked, wanting to confirm the miracle.

She laughed. The angelic voice of her laughter resonated through the room, making him smile unknowingly. Dead or not, his Apoorva was here, with him. And he would go to hell and beyond to stay with her forever. Ben watched as she leaned down and whispered in his ears, "Come with me, Ben?"

Where? He wanted to ask. But he didn't. Not everyone got a chance to meet up with their loved ones after death. He was one lucky man to have gotten this chance. He didn't want to ruin that. What if she leaves forever and never looks back if he asks something? He didn't want that. He would follow her to the deepest pits of hell if it meant staying with her. With no help, he sat up on his bed and reached out for his walker, wanting to go after Apoorva, who now waited near the door with a smile. He pranced across the room with everything in him. Apoorva opened the door and skipped forward, leading them to the stairs. Without questioning her actions, he followed, mesmerised by the contagious excitement in her movements. Two flights of stairs later, they were on the terrace of the hospital building as the night sky smiled down on them. Her eyes were fixated on the starry sky; her back was turned to him.

"Apoorva, baby, why did you leave me?" he asked, his throat constricting with pain. She didn't reply. He was not sure if she heard his question. "Apoorva..." he called out once again. Her eyes never left the starry dome above them as she spoke. "The night sky is so beautiful. Right, Ben? The specks of gold manning it make it even more beautiful. Do you think there's anything more beautiful than this night sky?" Ben stood there, dumbfounded, not knowing what to say. She turned towards him, her eyes shining with love. "Obviously there are things more beautiful than this. You must be thinking, What? Your love, Ben. Pure, unaltered love. Nothing in this life could be more beautiful to me than your love for me," she said. Her voice was so calm that it brought some peace to his chaotic mind. She valued his love like no other. He felt elated that she understood his devotion to her. God only knew how much he loved her.

She was standing right there, smiling innocently. Her skin sparkled under the moonlight, a few strands of air escaping from her braid in the wind. Yet she looked no less than an angel to him. He walked towards her with the help of his walker and put an arm around her. She leaned into his chest as a sigh of contentment escaped his lips. It must be unbelievable to others, but he knew that this was real. Apoorva was here, in his arms. He pressed his lips to her forehead, feeling the warmth of her skin against his lips.

Suddenly, she pushed out of his arms and ran towards the edge of the terrace. "Come with me, Ben. Don't spend your life alone. If you come with me, I'll be there with you for eternity," she said, stretching her arms out.

"But why would you want to leave here, Apoorva? Stay here, with me. I promise you. I will never fail you again. I'll guard you with my life." he said, making her drop her hands. She frowned, as if in contempt.

"I know, it must be difficult for you to leave this place for me. But I had hoped you would. Don't worry, I'll leave you alone." she said, turning away from him.

No, baby, I didn't mean it like that. Please don't go," he pleaded after her. She once again turned towards him, a sad smile on her lips. "I can't stay here forever, Ben. My time here is limited. If you come with me, we will have all the time in the world together," she said.

Ben looked at her helplessly, weighing his options. He wanted nothing more than to be with her. As he thought, she said, "We are getting late, dear. Make your choice now, as I don't have much time left." What was he even waiting for? He knew that he would gladly leave this world if it meant having Apoorva with him forever. He slid his hand into hers; their grip was firm. Hand in hand, they walked towards the edge of the terrace. One step more, and he could escape this world with her. As he tried to take a step forward towards his liberation, someone pulled him back. "What the hell are you doing, son?" a voice asked. He looked to his side. Apoorva was no longer there. His palms were cold from the windy night. He looked before him to see that he was standing on the top of a 100-foot-high building. A step more, and he would fall into nothingness. Ben couldn't believe it. He was going to commit suicide? His breaths started coming out in short laboured heaves, as he turned around and looked at his saviour. A middle-aged man held his collar, stopping him from walking further. Sweat beads formed on his forehead and neck as he thought about what would have gone wrong if the man hadn't seen him. His palm was clammy, and his limbs were shivering. He tried to speak, but nothing came out. Darkness overtook his senses before he could do anything.

A few days later, Ben was discharged from the hospital. He could walk without a walker and do everything on his own. When he reached home, Jeff was waiting for him on the porch. "Good to have you back, buddy," Jeff said, patting him on the back. Once he reached his room, he sat down on his bed as Jeff arranged his things in the room. Ben started talking with no introduction. "The pain. It is too much. The vile grip that it has over my heart is unbearable. I am unable to forget." Jeff sighed. He left what he was doing and walked to Ben, making him stand. "Let's go out for a coffee," he said, dragging his friend outside. Jeff drove, while Ben sat in the passenger seat, peering out of the window. His thoughts were filled with Apoorva. They always were. Memories seemed to imprison him whenever he tried to escape. His attempts to flee were also named after him.He didn't want to escape them, for all that was left were those memories. The ride was mostly silent. Jeff occasionally cracked some jokes to catch his attention. Ben would smile reluctantly, as if he were forcing himself to do so. After some time, Jeff gave up, leaving Ben once again to his thoughts. As the silence stretched on, Jeff's phone rang. He swerved the vehicle into a clearing and took the phone. It was his mom. She wanted him to go home as his grandma was having difficulty breathing. Jeff drove back to his house with Ben to check on her.

"What happened, mom? She was alright when I left." Jeff asked, as soon as he kept his foot in the foyer.

His mom came out, panicking. "I don't know, son. I was in the kitchen making breakfast for her. But then she started calling out for me as if in pain. I don't know what to do. That's why I called you. The woman sobbed into Jeff's chest, holding him close.

Wiping his mom's tears, Jeff rushed into his grandma's room, with Ben tagging along. She was lying on the bed, breathing heavily. As Ben watched, tears gathered in Jeff's eyes. The same Jeff who would crack jokes about how the entire world is a happy place The same Jeff who acted like a joker around his friends

"Let's take her to the hospital, ma. I don't know what else to do. Every second we spend here may cost us her life." Jeff said as he started to gather the frail woman in his hands.

"Jeff, relax," Ben said, making Jeff turn towards him. His eyes were puffy, and tears were flowing out of them.

"How can I relax, Ben? Can't you see? She is struggling. I can't just sit back and do nothing." Jeff said, once again turning back to the struggling woman.

"Calm down, Jeff." Let's take her to the car. We will go to my parents' hospital, okay?

"By the time Jeff and his mom wheeled his grandmother out, Ben was in the driver's seat, ready to drive. He knew that Jeff wouldn't be able to drive safely with so much tension. It was his first time behind the wheel after losing Apoorva. But he knew that he had to overcome his fears. Situations like these demanded it out of him. So he was going to do better. If not for him, then for the people around him who loved him dearly, for their benefit.

They reached the hospital in less than 10 minutes. The ailing woman was taken to a hospital emergency room and given proper treatment, bringing her back to life.

Jeff and Ben walked out of the building to the hospital garden. Ben was eyeing the flowers with keen interest, while Jeff was looking elsewhere. "You know what, Jeff? I could never forget Apoorva. Even these flowers remind me of her." Ben said, looking at the rose flowers.

"Who asked you to forget her? No one, Ben. Forgetting her would be a sin. I just want you to move on. These memories will keep you going till the end. Move on. That's it. Drowning in sorrow will get you nowhere. She'll not come back if you live your life like this. Please understand that." Jeff said, his eyes pleading for his friend to see reason.

Days passed by. Ben would rarely leave his room or talk to others. Sometimes, Jeff would visit him and drag him out for a drive. Throughout the drive, he would give long speeches about how life should go on, no matter what storm struck. No word of his really touched Ben's heart. His mind was still revolving around Apoorva's death and how she was gone and would never come back. Staying in his room alone for so long was starting to take a toll on him—both mentally and physically. His facial hair was overgrown. His skin was sickly pale, and his limbs were lanky. Nightmares haunted his sleep, making him sleepless.

Apoorva barreled into his life with no notice and left just like that. A rainbow that showed him how beautiful and addictive love can be— that was her. It was as if she never existed and that everything else was just a dream. People say that when our loved ones leave this world, they appear as stars in the sky to watch over us. If she was watching him, he wanted to tell her that he was not okay without her. That he was hanging by a thread between life and death. That the memories she gifted him were haunting him, making him wish for more for her. If the myth were true, he was sure that she would be the brightest star in the sky.

That year, the monsoon arrived early. Day and night were alike—cold, windy, and cloudy, just like his mind. As the thunderstorm stuck, his mind too was in an uproar. The angry swing of trees was similar to the duel of thoughts going on in his mind. He looked out of the window, watching the angry dance of nature. When he turned around, he could see his own reflection looking right at him. At first, he thought it was the mirror. Later, he realised that it was not. It was him. His own self It was looking at him with pity.

"What are you waiting for?" his voice asked him. The voice was so soothing, yet addictive. "End this pain," it whispered once again. Ben listened to the voice with so much interest. "Suicide. That is your only option. Liberate yourself. It'll hurt only a bit. But after that, you'll never know that feeling again. Do it."

His heart was thumping loudly. His mind was in a tug of war between life and death. Why would he choose life? His life had no meaning without Apoorva in it. Death could liberate him and unite him with her. That's what he had always wanted. In no time, he made a knot and put it around his neck. The other end was tied to the clamp on the ceiling. He closed his eyes to stop thinking about the choices that made him want to live and to focus on everything that death had to offer. He was about to kick the chair from under his legs when he saw Max standing on the ground, whimpering at his self-destructive self. The vulnerable look in that animal's eyes thinned his resolve to die as he untied the knot and stepped down, holding the pup close. He cried into his fur, making the animal whimper at every sob of his. Ben couldn't help but recall the day they got him. How could he? It was one of the most beautiful days of his life. That day, he spent every moment with Apoorva. And Max had been her gift to him for everything he had done for her. Max was their gift. The pup was a witness to the love they had for each other.

Whenever Apoorva and Ben wanted to spend some quality time together, they always chose someplace close to nature. Somewhere far from the hustle and bustle of the city, where they had no qualms about stares, A place where the internet connection is weak and the heart-to-heart connection is strong.

Apoorva and Ben had been to such a place once. It was their brief escape from monotonous city life and the corporate rat race. With them both working for different corporations in two different parts of the city, they barely had any time to meet each other, and chats over the phone were their only mode of communication. The weekend getaway to 'Paradise of Love' was Apoorva's idea. The place was 3 hours away from the city by road. The place was well known for the beautiful heart-shaped pond on the top of a mountain, which is made from the natural stream of a gigantic waterfall. It also had two huge rocks in the middle of the pond with something carved on their tops. Locals believe it to be the name of the prince and princess who discovered this secret place and sat on these rocks daily for hours and hours and dreamt of their 'Together and Forever'. They fought alongside their fathers, who were Great Kings and mortal enemies.

Another myth that surrounded the pond was that there was a princess who dreamed about a heart-shaped pond. No matter how hard she tried, she couldn't find the pond anywhere in her kingdom. So she proclaimed to the people of her country that she'd marry the man who would find the pond. There was a poor man in the village who was secretly in love with the princess. Because he was not rich, he knew that his love for the princess would never come true. When he heard this news, he went on a journey to find the pond. Even after searches that extended over days, he couldn't find the pond. But he never gave up. His love for the princess was stronger than that. After a search that lasted over 500 days, he discovered the pond and went to the palace to inform the princess of his discovery. The princess was very happy. Impressed by his dedication, she agreed to marry the man. Though the King was not happy with the alliance, they fought against all the odds together and got married. Thus, the poor man was crowned King of the Kingdom. After their marriage, both of them would visit the pond every day and stay there for hours. In the end, they died in each other's arms while sitting on the rocks at the centre of the pond.

No matter which story people believed the most, the place was a lover's paradise. People like him and Apoorva, who wanted a break from the chaos of city life, would visit this place.

Both the stories were too cheesy for Ben to believe. He was sure that these were all the myths propagated by the locals to gain more attention from the city folk. Yet when Apoorva said she wanted to visit the pond, he couldn't say no. Her happiness meant the world to him. Just like the locals, she too believed that amidst the forest, with so many turns and diversions, if you could find this place without any help, your love would be eternal, just like that of the prince and princess.

That day, they started their ride at 5 in the morning. She was so excited to find the place. She chattered nonstop about the photos they'd take and upload on Instagram. Ben, on the other hand, was worried sick. This place was located somewhere in the middle of a forest. What if there were wild animals? What if they couldn't find the place before sunset? What if they couldn't find the place at all? What if they lost their way and got stuck in the forest? His worries knew no bounds, yet he was unable to share them with her. Her childlike excitement was too precious to be broken before even giving it a try. He also knew what would happen if they didn't find the damned place on their own. She'd go crazy, thinking that their love was not enough.

He was so immersed in his thoughts that he didn't hear Apoorva screaming in his ears.

"Bennnn........" he heard her call.

"Yeah?" he asked absentmindedly.

"Aaggghhh. Why are you so quiet? We came on this ride to get away from everything. Despite being physically present here, your mind is not here with me. What is the reason? Care to share?" she asked, annoyance clear in her voice.

"I was just admiring nature." "It's so different from what we are used to," he said, trying to divert her attention.

"Liar, liar, pants on fire. I know you better than this, Ben. Now tell me what is bothering you." She demanded, refusing to let go of the matter.

Ben knew that he couldn't escape now. Why did he even think that Apoorva wouldn't catch his lies? What she said was right. She knew him better than himself.

He explained how he was worried about bug bites, darkness, and not finding the pond.

"What did you think? That I was not worried about all these?" she asked, after he shared his worries list with her. "Do you know what's in my backpack? I brought a first-aid kit, torches, batteries, power banks, snacks, and an extra pair of shoes for both of us. I didn't venture on this journey without thinking anything through, Ben. Moreover, if we don't find the place before five in the evening, we can come back. I'll argue no more," she said, smiling brightly.

On hearing her words, the wrinkles on his face were completely replaced by a full-blown smile.

"Wah... you are a gem, my baby," he said, glancing at her through the rearview mirror.

Oye, mister, now stop with your cheesy dialogues and concentrate on your driving," she said, playfully glaring at him through the mirror. They rode forward, feeling the gentle breeze caressing their bodies, giving them a fresh feeling. The air was so fresh that he just wanted to stop there and never return to the city.

When they reached the foot of the mountain that they were supposed to climb, Ben was awestruck by the sheer beauty of nature. "Look how beautiful this place is. If I had a choice, we would never leave this place. Look at those mountains. Their peaks look like they are kissing the clouds." Ben said enthusiastically, pointing his finger to some faraway mountain. Apoorva was amused by his childlike excitement. She smiled, patting him on his shoulder.

"That's enough gawking for now. There are more beautiful scenes on our way up there." She pointed up. "And hurry up. We don't have much time left."

According to the information available on Google, it'd normally take 3 hours of ascent and 2 hours of descent. They had planned to return by 5 in the evening. It was also said that there were two other waterfalls on the same mountain. By chance, if you lost your way and ended up near some other waterfall, it'd be even harder to find your way back. A local guide's help was advised if they wanted to reach the pond without fail. But being the stubborn girl and hopeless romantic that Apoorva was, she refused to take the help of a local guide. She wanted to find the paradise of love on her own.

An hour into their expedition, they had passed so many trees and bushes. The lanes were narrow and covered with dry leaves. Ben was on the front, guiding her forward. They were trudging along a narrow path that had a cliff to his right when Ben's feet slipped. He would have fallen off the cliff if not for Apoorva's presence of mind. She held his hand tightly and pulled him towards the other side, pulling him away from death itself.

Ben stood up and dusted himself. His eyes darted to Apoorva's fear-stricken face. She was looking at him as if she had seen a ghost. Trying to lighten the mood, he said, "Normally, the hero saves the heroine. But look at us, it is my superwoman who saved me from death." He laughed, hoping for her to catch on to the joke.

"You..." she started, pointing her finger at him. "This is not a joke, Ben. For a moment, I forgot to even breathe. For a moment, I thought I had lost you. Couldn't you just walk cautiously? And, on top of that, you are laughing. How could you...?" The rest of her rambling was silenced by a kiss from him. By the time his lips left hers, she was sobbing with a baby in his arms. He held her close, whispering sweet nothings in her ear.

"How can I die, leaving you alone here? I could never do that. We have a lifetime together to celebrate our love. No one can rob us of it." he said, kissing her forehead. He took his handkerchief and wiped her tears, her sobs subsiding with each caress of his.

She then smiled brightly at him. A full-blown smile that promised him all the happiness in the world. At that moment, he wondered how someone could be this beautiful. Apoorva wore no jewellery. Not even an earring. Her doe eyes were lined with a simple stroke of kohl. Her long, wavy hair was held up in a tight bun. Yet with no makeup, she looked ethereal.

"I know that. After all, when this superwoman is right here with you, what could go wrong?" she laughed, throwing her head back.

"Ah, that was enough to feed your ego for one day. Let's start moving." Ben said, pulling her along with him. Hand in hand, they resumed their journey, playing their favourite songs on the phone. On their way, they flirted with each other like teenagers.

"Yuhi katt jaayega safar sath chalne se... Manzil aayegi nazar saath chalne se. La la la la la," hummed Apoorva.

"Roop tera mastana, pyaar mera deewana,bhool koi humse na hojaye," teased Ben with a mischievous smile on his face, which made Apoorva blush.

Love is a responsibility. A responsibility that weighs down on the two people involved. Apoorva and Ben did their parts very well in their journey. They were each other's support system no matter what came their way. They were laughing, teasing, jumping, resting, and enjoying each other's company like never before. It made them realise that their love was not lost. Their love has not lost its charm but has just grown mature enough to understand each other's silence. For them, love was their salvation, the only constant in the ever-changing course of life. On their way, they clicked as many photos as they could. Apoorva defined photographs as a way to stop time and a way to store away memories. When put that way, he just couldn't stop her from clicking pictures. They walked for what felt like an eternity. Somewhere at a distance, they could hear the sound of a waterfall. They picked up their pace and walked in the direction of the sound, hoping to find the pond soon. They came across a bridge that looked like it would fall off at any moment. Hand in hand, they crossed the bridge, holding each other tightly. Once they crossed the bridge completely, Apoorva picked up her pace once again and dragged Ben with her, excited to find the heart-shaped pond. Soon they found the waterfall but realised that it was not the one they were looking for.

Apoorva's dejected face was a clear indication of how disappointed she was. Though finding the pond was of no importance to him, Apoorva's sad face pained him to no end. Unknowingly, deep down in his heart, he too wanted to find the 'paradise of love'. His eyes were burning, gradually spreading the wetness of tears over them.

"I am sorry, Apoorva. I know how badly you wanted this. I am so sorry, my love, for disappointing you." He said this as tears gathered in his eyes.

Apoorva noticed his tearful eyes, which held so much pain behind them. Yes, she was disappointed that they couldn't find the pond. But she didn't believe, even for a second, that their love wasn't enough. She knew that it was. No matter what the myth told her, she knew that their love was ethereal. That it'd survive all the odds. She cupped his face with her palms and made him look into her eyes. "Look at me, Ben," she said, trying to make him see reason. "My paradise of love is you, Ben. No matter what the myths and legends say, you are my everything. So what if we didn't find the pond? Does that mean that our love is any less? No, Ben. Our love is eternal. We don't need to find a stupid pond to prove that." His head rested against hers, their hands interlocked. "This was what I desired. Your company, our memories, and this peacefulness Nothing more." she continued. Closing her eyes, she pressed a chaste kiss to his lips, making him forget his sorrows. Yes, it was their happiness that mattered. He needed no more evidence for their ethereal love. Only Apoorva's opinion mattered. Nothing else.

Their moment of peace was disturbed by a small bark. They looked for the source of the barking and saw a cute little puppy standing there, looking alone and broken. He inched closer to them as if dreading an attack from them. When they made no move to harm him, he started jumping around, as if to showcase his smarts before them. Something about him made Apoorva want to take him home. She looked at Ben with puppy eyes, asking for permission. When she made a move to catch him, he ran away from them, stopping at a distance. Apoorva ran behind him, chasing him to a clearing. He stopped there, letting her feed him biscuits. When she looked above, she saw a signboard with an arrow sign. "Paradise of love—5 minutes," it read, making her jump up and down with happiness. She went back to where Ben was sitting and dragged him to the clearing, all the while carrying the puppy in her arms. Ben was also elated to find the pond. He now had no problem bringing the pup back home, as it showed them the way to their destination. Following the sign, they found the pond that they were looking for nearby.

"Look at that, Ben. We found the pond. We found the paradise of love. Our love is too eternal. Just like that of the poor man and the princess," she said, bubbling with happiness. After clicking a bunch of pictures together, they decided to go back. They let the puppy lead the way. By the time they reached the foot of the mountain, it was dark.

Their ride back home was much cheerier than the former one. The little bundle of joy that now Apoorva held in her hands was in no mood to stay quiet. He barked happily in her arms, feeling the cool gush of air against his furry body.

"What should we name him, Ben?" Apoorva asked, glancing at him through the rear-view mirror.

"This puppy led us to our destination. He was the reason for our maximum enjoyment. So, let's name him Max." He suggested it, winking at her through the rearview mirror.

"Wow... nice name. So you are Max from now on," she said, patting the puppy on its head.

That's how Max came into their lives. This pup was a witness to how they loved each other unconditionally. He was there with them on almost every trip they went on. How could he just forget Max and take his life for his own selfish reasons? Ben was ashamed for giving into the evil temptation even for a moment. He couldn't do that to his loved ones. They loved him to no end. He couldn't leave all that just to escape from all his miseries. Max was a memory that Apoorva gifted him. He was determined to live the rest of his life happily with those memories. He knew that Apoorva would have wanted that if she were alive. He pushed all his negative thoughts aside and went to sleep, hoping to find a new purpose for his life.

She vanished into the waves of clouds

Left him alone in this ill-favoured world.

His soul is sold and served to rot,

His lungs couldn't take or hold his breath.

She just left without a bye,

His eyes wandered around

Flooding his face.

There their journey has come to an end.

PART 6

I sat back and watched the birds head back to their homes in flocks. Their silhouette falling against the twilight sky was rather refreshing. The calm that nature painted annoyingly rivalled the turmoil in my heart, clinging to my chest like a persistent anchor. The tug was so strong that I feared if I tried to pull away, it'd take a piece of my heart with it. I waited for Jeff to go on. Every word that I heard of Ben came out like it was coming from a sinking ship—inexplicably heart-wrenching. I had no desire to meddle in tragedies; I'd stay far away from those in any way possible. Yet, with Ben and his life, I couldn't do that. I wanted to know more about his life and how he fared with all their beautiful memories haunting him. God knows what I would do if something happened to April. I loved April with every fibre of my being, and losing her would push me into the darkest abyss of self-destruction. What Ben went through touched me oddly, in a sense that is so familiar yet haunting, as I was no stranger to love, the feeling that bares us unguarded.

Jeff sat on a bench behind me, watching every move of mine. I paced around, Ben's pain flowing into me and scalding me like red-hot lava. On the table were two bowls of Khao Suey, left untouched and cold. The sun was setting into the sky, colouring the waters in the brightest hue of orange. I was now more impatient than ever to hear the rest of what happened. Exhaling, I mustered all the courage left in me and turned back to Jeff with a nod.

Apoorva's loss shattered Ben in the most irreparable ways. Grief ate him from the inside; the once sunny face of a young man was now replaced with a hollow shell of a man who would barely fit the description. His days started with her tombstone, morphing into unproductive days and sleepless nights. Letters exchanged between them were now engraved in his mind. Not a day passed without him reliving the nightmare, making him curse himself. He fell into a slumber of agony and self-loathing. Wherever he went, her memories followed him, haunting and mocking him, challenging every move of his. Memories gradually became a burden he could no longer bear.He refused to share his anguish with Jeff and even locked himself in his room. Anything anybody said to him fell on deaf ears. Memories enslaved him, their control over him getting stronger every day. Ben spiralled down, unable to take the grief anymore and finding salvation in drugs and alcohol. The insobriety they provided would make everything normal for some time, pushing him further down the abyss once the effect wears off. Little by little, his intake of the intoxicants increased, with any effort to pull him away by his family and friends failing miserably. He lived in a world of his own, with the name Apoorva never leaving his lips and her smile never leaving his mind. The more Jeff tried to keep him on track, the more he slipped away, refusing to accept help, drowning himself, yet bouncing back to the surface gasping for breath, only to torment himself more.

Jeff sat under a tree, watching the setting sun. The state his friend was in worried him a lot. Though he has known him only for a few years, Ben holds a special place in his heart. The path his friend is now traversing was something he never expected Ben to choose. Ben loved Apoorva so much that she was the centre of his universe. Apoorva's tragic death shook his entire world, pushing him off the cliff of life. Ben's condition was so bad that Jeff feared that someday he'd slip past a point of no return. As Jeff's thoughts took a turn towards more dreadful trajectories, his phone rang, indicating a call from Ben's mother. The woman who once greeted him with warm smiles and lovely laughter was now crying over the phone. Her concern for her son poured over the call, her sobs, wreaking havoc in his soul. He ended the call with a promise to bring the old Ben back to life, regardless of the challenges he might face. He then left to find Ben, to talk some sense into his now-slipping-away friend.

Jeff knew where to find Ben. After the misfortune, Ben was either in his room or the accident spot. Jeff reached the place to find a very tired Ben sitting under the tree, looking like a ghost of what he used to be. His eyes now had bags under them, and his body looked like he hadn't eaten in weeks. His once-shiny hair was now matted with dirt, and his 5 o'clock shadow was now replaced with an overgrown beard. Ben, who once looked like the epitome of perfection, was gone with Apoorva. Jeff was not sure if he'd ever get his friend back.

Parking his bike to the side, he walked to his friend, who, on hearing the sound of his footsteps, looked over. Ben's eyes roamed over Jeff, who sat down beside him, saying nothing. Both of them looked ahead, watching the sun go down on the horizon.

"What are you doing to yourself, Ben? This is not you. I want you back, Ben. I can't see you like this." Jeff said, not taking his eyes off the horizon.

"Why am I even breathing? I should've died. She deserved to live, love, and laugh. She shouldn't have died. We deserved much more." Ben sobbed into his hands, unable to control the tears anymore. Jeff held him close in an attempt to calm him down, which made Ben break into loud cries. Jeff's own eyes brimmed with tears, his friend's misery getting to him. "Calm down, Ben. Don't do this to yourself. You have us all. Apoorva wouldn't want this for you." Jeff said, hoping to calm him down.

"Can't you understand? She's not here. I don't want to live anymore." Ben yelled, pushing his friend away, his eyes spitting fire.

Jeff held his shoulders and shook him. "Don't you see me? Your mom? Your family? We all love you. We can't just stand there and watch you kill yourself little by little. You have a whole life ahead of you. Yes, Apoorva is no more. Does that mean you have to kill yourself? No. Respect her dreams and your memories together. Think back and ask yourself, Would she want this for you? You know the answer. She would want you to be sober and happy. She'd want you to be a good man; she always believed you were. Life is not easy. Apoorva was your everything. We all know that. Forgetting her is not an option. Memories will always stay with you, no matter what. But they should not haunt you. They should remind you about the good times you spent together. Think. Think. Your mom is always crying. Her eyes are always tearful. Not a day goes by without her calling and asking me to take care of you. Believe me, Ben. Let go of the grief. It'll get better. You'll learn to live with the memories. I need my friend back. Your mom needs her son. Please, Ben. Please come back to us." Jeff cried, hugging him tightly.

Even if it cost him his life, Jeff would still save his only friend. That's something he could live with, something he could carry to the end.

Jeff brought Ben back to his house. His mom came down and hugged her child, both of them shedding tears of happiness. He then went to his room for a shower. The woman held Jeff's hands, thanking him for his efforts. That night, Ben came down and had dinner with his family and Jeff. His hair was now combed back, the healthy shine of it returning. The beard that marred his beauty was now cut off, his signature 5 o'clock shadow back in its place. Though little, he talked to his family and began shaking the hands extended towards him, taking a step and giving a smile, like a baby learning the world anew.

Back in his room, he stared out of the window, watching the twinkling stars. Jeff entered the room, closing the door behind him.

"Look at that bright star, Jeff," Ben said, not taking his eyes off the night sky. "It must be her. It has to be her. It is the brightest star in the sky. She must be looking down on me, right, Jeff? What would she think of the man that I have been these past few days, Jeff? Will she hate me? I could never stand her hatred for me, Jeff. This is for her. This transition is just for her, Jeff. I don't want her to hate me. All this is for her." Ben muttered, flickering away the unshed tears.

"She could never hate you, Ben. She loved you so much. She would be very happy with the man that you chose to be." Jeff said, trying to convince his friend.

"You know what, Jeff? Now, when I try to recall that day's events without my guilt and emotions clouding my judgement, I feel like something is not right. We should go back to that place once again, Jeff. Please come with me," he pleaded.

"For what? You were in a very bad place, Ben. We thought you'd never return. Going back there will only pull you back. And what's the need? Police were there, and onlookers were there. There was nothing odd about it. Stay here for a few days. Talk to me, your family, and your friends. You'll feel much better. Once you have fully recovered from the trauma, we can go back there, okay?" Jeff replied, not wanting his friend to relive the tragic moment.

"Please, Jeff. Once is all I ask. Apoorva is a very careful rider. She rides safely. It was not us. Please believe me, Jeff. This is not trauma. Just for my peace of mind, please, Jeff. Please come with me." Ben pleaded, looking at his friend with tearful eyes.

"Okay. okay. Just this one time. I'll go with you. For this one time, I'll do whatever you want. But, after this, you'll listen to me. okay?" Jeff complied.

"Okay. Okay." Ben nodded, complying with his conditions.

The very next day, Jeff and Ben went to the accident spot. After surveying the area, Ben said, pointing to the nearby sweet shop, "Let us go there."

Jeff followed behind Ben, watching his every move like a hawk. Ben went to the shop and talked to the manager. In exchange for a few currency notes, he led both of them to the surveillance room and retrieved the CCTV footage of the fateful day. Watching the scene play out was more difficult than Ben expected. It reminded him again and again of how helpless he was. It was the one moment when everything he thought he accomplished in his life came down to nothing. He could feel his eyes burning. His hands were clammy. His legs felt like they were giving out. He gripped the nearby table hard, hoping to find some sort of support. He felt like vomiting, watching the visuals again and again. "This was not an accident. He did this intentionally." He mumbled to himself. So he wrote down the van's number and left the shop, not bothering to say anything. Jeff followed closely behind, suspicious about Ben's motives. Once they both were buckled in, Jeff asked, "What are you up to? Why did you take down the van's number?" Ben said nothing and stared out of the window, trapped in his thoughts throughout the drive.

Ben has always been a happy guy. The world has always been kind to him, except for Apoorva. The void that Apoorva left in his heart and life was huge and beyond repair. As he drove to his destination the very next morning, looking dapper, his mind was all taken up by a storm. Nothing he'd do will bring her back. He knew that. The least he could do for her soul and the peace of his mind was to find out the truth and bring the offender to justice. Ben was now on a mission to find the people who were responsible for his loss. He had already spent 3 months mourning over his loss, doing nothing. He now wanted to do something that'd make a difference.

His first destination was Apoorva's home, where he met Annie at the gate, as planned before. Annie gave him Apoorva's phone, which he used to retrieve the details of the calls she made that day. From the motor vehicle department's website, he collected the name and details of the van owner, who turned out to be the owner of a rental car showroom.

Ben visited the rental car showroom and met with the owner. The owner was a kind old man who chatted with him like a good old friend.

"So uncle." Ben started. "A friend of mine rented this car from your shop last week, and now his ID card is missing. I think it'll be in there somewhere. Could you please check?" He asked, sounding harmless.

"We always check the cars for anything left behind by customers when we take the vehicle back. I don't think it'll be there in the car." The old man replied kindly.

But, uncle, could you please search the van for reassurance? His ID is lost, and you know how complicated this paperwork can get if you apply for a new one. If you check there once, we could cut out the chances of losing it here." Ben pressed politely, trying not to get in his way.

The old man finally nodded, asking Ben for the number of the vehicle. Ben ratted out the number of the van that caused their accident. When asked for the date, Ben asked for the registration book to confirm the date. The owner brought the logbook out for him to inspect. Ben then pointed to some random date on which the same van was rented by someone else, convincing the owner to check the vehicle. While he went out to search for the ID, Ben took his phone out and snapped a photo of details concerning the person who rented the van on the day of their accident. He then set the logbook back in its place and waited for the owner of the shop to return.

"Son," the man called. Ben left the cabin and met him outside, near the car. "See? Your friend's ID is not here." He pointed to the car. "We always check for anything left behind by the customers," he said, making Ben roll his eyes.

"I'm so sorry, uncle, for the inconvenience I caused." He apologised and left the shop. The second stage of Ben's investigation included studying the routine of the person who rented the van that day. He was a truck driver who'd visit the cheapest bar in the city every night for his fill of alcohol. He'd leave the bar by the middle of the night, wasted and crawling.

After a week of thoroughly observing the man, on a Sunday night, Ben went to the bar. The insides of the bar reeked of cheap alcohol, cigarettes, and sex. Ben studied his surroundings. People were drinking and celebrating like nothing was wrong, feeling up the bodies of the waitresses passing by. Disgust coursed through his veins, making it difficult for him to walk any further. His rationale came to his rescue, reminding him of his purpose, Apoorva. Ben marched forward and sat down near the counter, ordering a whisky. A woman came near him, smelling like cigarettes and cheap alcohol, and delivered his drink. He refused to glance her way and took his drink, muttering a simple thank you. The woman stayed beside him for some time, touching him and asking a few questions, to which he paid no heed. Finally, when her company got unbearable, he glared her way, making her scurry away from his vicinity.

Ben watched silently as the man who had crushed his life entered the bar. His fists clenched at his sides in an attempt to contain his anger. The man came forward and sat near Ben. He ordered his usual and took a puff of his already-lit cigarette. A few minutes later, a woman came, carrying his order. Ben watched as the man extended his hands to fondle the woman, who seemed to enjoy his lustful touches. He took a swig of his drink and exhaled loudly, ordering more with a wave of his hand. In an hour, he was almost wasted and spewing bullshit out of his mouth. His touches on the waitresses' bodies became more violent and desperate, making the girl shake away from his hold. Ben watched as he stood up, feeling his own pockets for his purse, and swayed towards the washroom. Ben followed him silently and entered the washroom with him, closing the door behind him. The man looked back, hearing the loud thud of the door, swaying on his legs. "Rich, aren't you?" The man slurred. Ben looked at him, disgust evident in his gaze. "Your looks and the clothes you are wearing scream money," the man continued. "Why would someone like you visit a bar like this? For sport? I am sure not," the man said, laughing like a maniac. "Got some dirty business?" he garbled again. "Give me money. I will do anything for you," the man mumbled incoherently, pressing his hand on the counter to straighten himself. Rage overtook Ben's composure as he swung his hand, landing a mean punch in the man's face. He fell, yelling and clutching his face. As the man struggled to get up from the ground, Ben crouched low before him, showing him the CCTV footage of the accident and the photo of the logbook at the rental car service. The man's eyes were clouded with fear, his cries subsiding in his throat.

"Remember this day?" Ben asked, rage clear in his voice. "I lost everything that gave meaning to my life on that day. If you make a sound, I will kill you. I have nothing more to lose. Give me the answers I need, and you can walk out of this room unharmed. If you try to act smart, mind me; I have nothing more to lose. I'll finish you in the blink of an eye." Ben said, his voice hard.

The man nodded, fear evident in his eyes, not making any noise.

"This accident was a planned one, isn't it?" Ben asked as the man nodded yes, too scared to speak up.

"Speak up. I don't want these nods. I need answers." Ben yelled, the thunderous boom of his voice making the man cower in fear. He nodded, too afraid to speak up.

Ben's fist collided with the wall, punching a hole through it. "I won't repeat." He muttered lowly.

"If you won't speak up, next time it will be your head I will punch a hole in," he said as the man started wailing loudly.

"Yes sir. yes. Somebody asked me to do this." The man said that his speech was now clearer than ever.

"Who?" Ben asked, his patience thinning out.

"I don't know." The man said, breathing heavily.

Ben let out an exhale of annoyance. The man was testing his patience. He didn't want to do anything rash. But only violence seemed to make the man in front of him speak. Ben pulled out a pocket knife from his slacks. The man in front of him started crawling back in fear, his hands flailing. The fear seemed to have a vile grip on his throat, as no sound came out of his mouth. His crawl stopped when his back met the wall. Tears rolled out of his eyes as he heaved repeatedly, trying to find his voice. Ben knelt down and said, "I told you I wouldn't repeat myself. Congrats!!! Your silence has earned you more pain." Ben's hand moved swiftly, splattering a fountain of blood on the floor. The man screamed, holding on to what was left of his left ear.

"Nobody is going to hear you. I'm sure about that. But I want you to stop screaming. You deserve the pain to eat you away in silence. I have endured a pain a thousand times greater than this in silence. There was no cure. For it pained my heart and not my body." Ben said, his voice calm.

The man continued to scream, his scared eyes never straying from Ben's vengeful ones. Blood from his ear flowed down into the drain as if it were a river.

"Stop screaming now or I won't hesitate to cut your other ear as well," Ben said, his tone void of any emotion.

The man's screams stopped instantly, transforming into hiccupping sobs. With his bloodied hands, he clutched his mouth tightly to muffle the noise.

"Now, now, don't do that. I want you to speak. I want you to tell me his name. Won't you do that for me?" Ben asked, a sinister smile playing on his lips.

The man's eyes widened. He shook his head no frantically.

"Believe me, denial is going to bring you more pain. So much pain that you'll hope for death more than life. But I won't let you. I won't let you die until you've suffered enough for the heinous crime you've committed." Ben's tone was now deadly, as if a storm was about to be unleashed.

"I don't know," the man bellowed out.

"Tsk... Tsk… You don't know? How could you not know?" Ben asked, mockery clear in his speech. "You know him well, and you are going to tell me his name," Ben said, the dangerous edge in his tone returning.

"I can't… I can't!" the man yelled out, as he held on to Ben's feet, begging for mercy. Looking up, he said, "He'll kill me. He will destroy me."

"If you won't speak, in the next few minutes you'll wish you were never born," Ben said, gripping his knife tighter.

"No. No. No Please." The man said, holding on to Ben's feet for dear life. "I'll speak. I'll speak." He said, gulping down.

"I don't know his name. He referred to the dead girl as his stepdaughter," the man mumbled in a whisper.

For a minute, Ben sat there, shocked. This was something he didn't expect. Yes, he knew that Apoorva's family hated her. But killing her? He didn't think their hatred would stretch to this extent.

"Did you see the man?" Ben asked, eyeing the bloodied man on the floor.

"Yes sir. Yes," the man said.

"Could you describe his features?" Ben asked cautiously, wanting to confirm his allegation.

"He was tall, lean, and fair. Wore spectacles. Had sharp eyes. I don't remember anything else." The man spoke, joining his hands in an attempt to excuse himself.

Ben stood up, anger consuming him and flowing through his veins like hot lava. Ben looked down at the man, who was pleading on his feet.

"How much did he pay?" Ben prodded.

"10 lakhs in cash," the man said, shedding tears, "please, sir, let me go. I have a family to feed." He held Ben's feet in an attempt to get him to forgive him.

"Didn't you think of my family when you killed my girl? Or did you think only you had a family?" Ben asked, kicking the man's hand away. Ben smashed his face on the counter and picked him up by his collar.

"Run… Run as fast as you can. Because once I settle this, I am coming for you. And then I'll end your miserable excuse of a life forever." Ben said, trampling the man's face under his boots.

Ben walked out of the washroom, leaving the man on the floor to deal with his fate.

That night, Ben didn't sleep. His mind was taken up by a storm. He repeated his dialogue for the next day again and again in his mind.

He tossed and turned restlessly the entire night, the events impending to unfold the very next day keeping him awake.

The next day, Ben decided to walk to Apoorva's house. He strolled down the alleyway, the scorching sun shining brightly above him, listening to the crunch of leaves under his feet. This visit was something he didn't look forward to, yet it was inevitable. As he neared her house, his heart started beating out of his chest, and sweat beads formed on his forehead. A heavy feeling settled in his chest, weighing him down and reducing his pace significantly. The gates were wide open. In the foyer, in an easy chair, sat the woman she called mother, some magazines resting on her lap, her eyes trained on the road ahead of her. She looked pale as a ghost, her once neatly combed black hair now sticking out in all directions as streaks of grey.

She didn't notice Ben entering the compound. Ben walked straight into her garden, which once bloomed flowers but is now a heap of dry leaves. Ben clearly remembered the day Apoorva showed him her garden. Ben was home after a long day and made a video call to Apoorva. When she picked up her head, her forehead was smudged with potting soil, and she was sweating profusely. But none of that seemed to deter her spirit. Her eyes were beaming with joy. She then gave him a detailed tour of her garden. He has never been a fan of gardening. But seeing her talk so excitedly about each plant and flower, he didn't have the heart to stop her. The way her face brightened when she talked about those plants was enough to refresh his mind, body, and soul. So he sat there, silent like an obedient child, hearing her blabber about it. Back then, butterflies of different colours flew freely around her, making her seem no less than an angel. The next day when they met, Apoorva had a pot of moss roses in her hand. When his quizzical gaze met hers, she had said, thrusting the pot into his hand. "This is my gift for you. Water it every day. Make sure that it gets enough sunlight, but not too much." His face would have looked comical to her then. She met it with a smile of her own and an encouraging pat on his back. A week later, when it withered out completely due to his neglect, Apoorva was upset beyond anything. She kept away from him for two days. Then only he understood how serious she was about her plants. But now, seeing all her love and hard work turn grey and colourless, he couldn't help but think of rebuilding its lost glory. Tears threatened to spill over as he exhaled loudly, trying to keep them at bay. He walked to the foyer, where Apoorva's mom sat, still unaware of his presence.

"Could you please stop this? I am not going to believe your tears after everything. How could you? How could you do this to her?" Ben yelled angrily, tears flowing down his cheeks. Apoorva's mom shifted in her seat, looking at him with tearful eyes.

"I didn't," the woman mumbled lowly. "I didn't do it."

"Please. Please don't lie to me. I know everything now. You may convince others with this drama. But, not me." Ben yelled again, his face red with anger.

"Ben," the woman started. "I don't deny the fact that I paid more attention to Annie once she was born. But that didn't mean that I loved her any less. She called me mom when I couldn't be one. She made me a mother. I could never scold her, let alone kill her. Please believe me. I didn't," she said, pleading with her eyes.

"Then how did you know that I was here to ask you this?" Ben asked, a disgusted look crossing his face.

"I know my husband did it. I heard him talking to the van driver while you were in the hospital." Her eyes held a sea of remorse, enough to haunt her for life.

"Then why didn't you report him to the police? If you loved her so much, why didn't you fight for justice?" Ben asked sarcastically.

"Because I'd lose my other daughter if I did that," she said, looking Ben straight in the eyes. "My husband did this in the name of Annie. He wanted Annie to be the centre of everyone's attention. So, when Apoorva started stealing the limelight with her warm heart and kind ways, he couldn't stand it anymore. Annie is still attending counselling sessions to overcome the grief of her sister's demise. If I let the world know this, she'd know too. With her current mental condition, she will blame herself and might even commit suicide. I have already lost one, Ben. I can't afford to lose the other one too." She sobbed, joining her hands before him.

Ben stood there, unable to speak anymore as the woman broke down in front of him.

"I know she was everything to you. That said, it'd be difficult, if not impossible, for you to move on. Believe me. After knowing the truth, my life has not been any less than hell. Every day, when I see Annie's face, I'm reminded of my apu. Every day, when I go to bed with that man, I feel dirty, like a traitor. All for my baby. I am letting everything pass just for Annie. Help me, Ben. I won't see another day if something happens to Annie. Please, son. Please let it pass for Annie." She sobbed, falling to his feet, her tears wetting his feet.

"I know you have your reasons. Appu was more than a girlfriend. I no longer have the zeal to live that I had while she was with me. However, I know that if she were here, she'd choose Annie over anybody else. So I will just let this go, even if it rips my heart apart to do so." Ben said and left, leaving her alone to ponder over her thoughts. He walked out of her house aimlessly, not sure where to go or what to do. It was as if nothing good was waiting for him down the lane of life. Unknown to his conscience, his feet carried him to Apoorva's tomb. Once there, he could no longer hold his tears back. His emotions got the best of him as he kneeled beside her, crying like a kid. "It was him, Appu. It was him all along. Your dad. How could he do this to you? How can someone be so cruel? I went there. I went there to confront him. But your mom!!! She stopped me. Begged me to spare him for Annie. I knew if you were here, you'd have chosen Annie and her happiness over anything else. So I could do nothing. Never in my life have I felt so useless. Knowing everything, watching him walk on the face of the earth happy till the end of his days, makes me want to give up on life." He lied down, his head resting on the tomb. "Lying here, just next to you, even if it is a graveyard, the world seems so bright. Without you, it is all dull and grey. Now tell me: how am I supposed to let someone like your dad roam free? He made my life a living hell. Say something, baby. It's been so long since I heard your voice." Ben closed his eyes, trying to control his tears. A soft touch on his cheek made him open his eyes. Running his hand over the face, he got hold of a white feather. Ben smiled wholeheartedly, something he hasn't done over the past few months. Holding the feather close to his heart, he said, "Is that your way of telling me that you have got your eyes on me from heaven? Thank you. Thank you so much. I could live on forever with this one belief." Ben stood up. Placing a silent kiss on the tomb, he walked away, the feather safe in his shirt's pocket.

Back home, he cried like a baby, letting the tears wash away his sorrows. He kept the feather inside his diary, safe from the outside world. When his tears dried down, Ben was sure of one thing: no matter what, his love for Apoorva wouldn't die. That no matter what, the passion and fire for her would stay ablaze no matter what his future beheld.

Ben's story evoked in me a pain that hurt, yet was nice to have. All I could do was pray for him to lead a better life and for her to find peace in the afterlife. According to Jeff, Ben's doing well now. He set up an NGO that worked day and night to eradicate hunger and illiteracy. They collected surplus food from hotels and party venues to distribute it among the poor. Besides that, they also made a book bank, where used books were stored and given to the needy. He was on a mission to eradicate everything that would pull people back from reaching for their dreams. Sure, it wouldn't be easy. He alone cannot change the world. But he was taking action. He was taking the first step, which many people never dared to take. He was living Apoorva's dream, keeping her alive through his good deeds. Her name was being uttered with happiness and gratitude; her short life is now a meaningful story to many. Ben too was living the best days of his life, finding happiness in others' smiles in Apoorva's name. He was slowly regaining his footing in this world, leaning on sweet memories and days that he hoped to be well spent.

That night, I drove home with a satisfied smile. Life was beautiful. Ups and downs were there, but not enough to make me quit. A life, no less than a dream, awaited me, embracing me with its warmth and making me shiver at the fear of losing it. I opened the windows of the car, the cold air gushing into the vehicle. My hair was tousled, and an odd feeling of calm coursed through my heart. I wanted to reach home as soon as possible, for my dream would wait for me there to numb my pain with a touch of hers.

I opened the door to my room. It was dark, and I turned the light on. I saw April standing near the balcony, enjoying the night sky. Unknowingly, a smile made its way to my face.

"Why are you staying in the dark, April?" I said, keeping the laptop bag on the table and sipping the water next to it.

"Sometimes it's beautiful to turn off all the lights and stay in the dark to escape from reality, even from our own shadow." She muttered and smiled widely, staring at the flower in her hand.

"That's the flower I gave you when we first met, right?" I asked him to undo my collar and doff my wristwatch.

"Yes, you have always had a great memory." She muttered, her eyes still lingering on the flower at hand.

My feet carried me towards her; my mind was no longer the master of my actions. My arms opened on their own accord, capturing her in a tight hug and caressing her rounded belly. My whole world now rested in my arms, and I could feel it pulling me into a sweet lullaby.

"Missed me, princess?" I asked playfully.

"Ha!!!! Look at you. You are finally free, yet you didn't call me." She complained, whining like a kid. Her eyes were fixated on the night sky, never leaving the view for even me.

"I got back just now. Ben's story was so disheartening that I needed some time to process it." I said it truthfully.

"Some days back we had a conversation about an important thing that happened in my life; do you remember?" April asked, turning towards me. Her eyes were shining, and the soft smile that I'd fallen in love with was never fading.

"How can I forget that? It was the sweet-and-sour day of my life," I said, adjusting her in my arms to accommodate the little human in her, between us.

Memories of the day started playing in my head, like scenes from a movie.

I was standing on the terrace, watching the colourful kites flying high in the evening sky. The children in our neighbourhood often spent their evenings like this. Kites of different colours and shapes flying high against the heavens were a beautiful sight to watch.

When I see those children, laughing with no care of the world, I realise that childhood is the most beautiful phase of one's life. Our lives are like that of kites'. We fly high; the sense of fear is unknown to us. Life becomes hell when you spend it with someone you don't love. Luckily, I had the best companion by my side—April.

No matter how I thought or how much I tried, I was still lost on how all this has changed Ben—to go through all this and stand his ground without falling apart. God knows how he holds it together. I cannot even begin to fathom the weight of losing everything I hold dear. To love someone with all you have, to long for someone to spend eternity with, and to not have them anymore in your life? God, for sure, is cruel.

As I wandered in my head, my thoughts took me back to April. *April.* I thought of her glossy eyes, with mischief in them, the way she stood beside me all this time, and how she kept me sane through all my mess.

What would it feel like for me to lose her? How would I feel if I woke up one morning to find her gone? Like she didn't exist in the first place? Or even worse, leaving behind a void I can never fill? An emptiness for an eternity to haunt me? Like a ghost of my lonely past? Like a persistent child tugging at the tunic of her mother for attention, what if the dreaded comes back to me?

"Pull yourself together". I chided myself.

My thoughts were interrupted by the sound of my phone ringing. I looked at the screen to see April's name flashing. Speak of the devil, and she shall call.

I picked up the phone to hear incessant sobbing from the other end. I couldn't even give her a formal greeting! I tried speaking, but her sobs didn't give me a chance. After what seemed like an eternity, her sobs started dying down, making me exhale in relief. This girl makes me do things I've never even dreamed of! Once her sobs turned into sniffles, I asked, "What happened, baby? Are you hurt or something?"

She heaved a long sigh. "Yeah! Something happened. And nothing is more important than that." She said, anger entering her tone. Her voice was no longer steady.

"What? Are you going to chop my magical wand for no reason?" I said, trying to tease her. Another sniffle came through, worrying me to no end.

"April? What happened? Are you alright? Do you want me to come there?" I asked as fear gripped my insides and my mind, making up a million negative scenarios.

"I lost the chain that you brought for me," she croaked through the phone, making my lips split into a wide grin.

"What? Is this true? When did you find out? Why are you even crying?" I ratted out in one go, feeling out of the blue.

"Because it was precious to me," she screamed through the phone. I was completely taken aback by the sudden shift in her mood. "I don't remember where I lost it or how it happened." She added.

"April, life offers us so much. But nothing lasts forever. Life herself takes it all out of our hands, often mercilessly. We humans never learn. Our desire for everything to be permanent is the cause of our sorrows. In due time, everything should leave behind its colour and become a faded memory." I said, trying to console her.

I was dragged back to reality when I felt her shuffling close to me on the balcony. My hands wrapped around her; my whole world was now resting against my heart.

"Look below us." She spoke. My eyes zeroed in on her fingers, which were pointing towards the well-lit city. "Below us, lights are being lit, cars are buzzing forward, and homes are alive with laughter and sorrows. There are many untold stories around us, written silently. Today, some were born, some met death, and some found love. There is always something or other happening around us. We cannot carry the burden of it all on our shoulders. Like the rest of the world, we will also row forward, trying to find a shore of happiness in this boat called life. As you mentioned in our last call, the things around us are ephemeral. Even the stars shining above us will wave goodbye to their glow one day. This cycle will go on until everything becomes a memory." Her arms tightened around mine. Our world is shrinking into us.

A hand on my shoulder made me jerk away from everything. Turning around, I saw my mom standing behind me, a light frown marring her face.

"Who are you talking to, son?" she asked, a soft smile replacing the frown. Her smile was so infectious that I met her face with a smile of my own. "No one," I said, making her shake her head.

"Come, Dinner's ready." She said so and turned away from me, leaving me to sink into the moment.

The harsh, cold wind greeted my hungry eyes and eager hands, making my heart wince at the chill. "I always thought having you next to me to narrate their story was a blessing. No one will ever understand me like you do, April. While you are indeed a blessing, I wish I had never met you. Because the more I think about you, the more I wish you were real, my love."

I know I will not lose her. I know for a fact that she will not leave me. *How?* You may wonder She is my fate, and I am hers. We're bound to one another like shadows to a body; even in the darkness, she doesn't leave me; she just spreads herself around. She watches over me, and I watch over her. I lean towards her, and she stretches her wings for me to take refuge. At this point, our worlds are so interconnected that the collapse of one will mean kaboom for the other as well.

Now that's a lot of trust to have in someone. You might think *Yes, it is.* How can I not when she exists just for me? When does her existence bore me to death? Only I hear her speak, giggle, and sigh; see her eyes sparkle; and feel her touch. *No,* she is not locked out in a cellar in the basement somewhere. She is somewhere *deeper and farther* than that. April lives in a place where there is *no escape;* it's a free place with no walls or doors to lock her in, and yet, she chose to stay. *Why?* I'll tell you why. Because it's me who created her, and she's all but real. Like a wish upon a shooting star, April is a fragment of my imagination, waiting to bloom into life. How can someone cease to exist if they never existed to begin with? I might be a madman for this, but isn't it better than drowning myself in grief and loss? *You tell me.*

Fluttering into my solitude it came,
Into a dry night, robbed off the stars-
An essence too free to tame,
Too real to be my imagination,
There it was, a butterfly-
I can't say it was my hallucination.

My thoughts don't rhyme anymore,
I speak in sighs of what's left,
I have got time on my hands,
And maybe, it was here to be friends.

Its legs perched on my finger,
I sat like a sad nomad under the starless sky-
Going on about like the ghost of Brown,
About and about my dramatic monologue.
There it was laid out, my life, like The Patriot and the My Last Duchess,
To be met with death at hands of the people I loved

A dry night and a scrapped sky,
Still, beauty shimmers from the little life wrapped around my finger.
I looked at it and maybe it looked at me.
It heard me whole or maybe didn't.
The wings fluttered again, and I felt lighter,
It had stops to make and I wasn't to stop.
The little thing then left as it came.